RAIN
of the
GHOSTS

RAIN
of the
GHOSTS

GREG
WEISMAN

 St. Martin's Griffin ☙ New York

This is a work of fiction. All of the characters, organizations, and events portrayed in this novel are either products of the author's imagination or are used fictitiously.

RAIN OF THE GHOSTS.
Copyright © 2013 by Greg Weisman. All rights reserved. Printed in the United States of America. For information, address St. Martin's Press, 175 Fifth Avenue, New York, N.Y. 10010.

www.stmartins.com

Design by Anna Gorovoy

Map by Rhys Davies

The Library of Congress Cataloging-in-Publication Data is available upon request.

ISBN 978-1-250-02979-9 (trade paperback)
ISBN 978-1-250-02980-5 (e-book)

St. Martin's Griffin books may be purchased for educational, business, or promotional use. For information on bulk purchases, please contact Macmillan Corporate and Premium Sales Department at 1-800-221-7945, extension 5442, or write specialmarkets@macmillan.com.

First Edition: December 2013

10   9   8   7   6   5   4   3   2   1

For Beth, Erin & Benny . . .

something to read together . . .

ACKNOWLEDGMENTS

Thanks to Jeffrey Katzenberg, Gary Krisel and Bruce Cranston for setting the stage for Rain's creation. (And to Kim Mozingo, Tanna Harris, Emily Gmerek and John Hardman for making that setting more fun.)

Thanks to John Skeel for developing Rain with me. To the conference room gang (Bruce Cranston, Darin Dusanek, Lydia Marano, John Skeel & Jon Weisman) for their help in fleshing out the concepts. And to Sam Bernstein for handing me the key to the last missing Ghost.

For help with research, I'd like to thank Darin again and John. Plus Wally Weisman, Chris & Steve Leavell, Jordan Mann and Jennifer Anderson. And thanks to Jennifer and Seth Jackson and the rest of the Gathering Players for allowing me to see Rain, Charlie and the rest live. Plus Lex Larson for providing the Cache, and Eirik Paye for help with the map. Also appreciated: Gorebash, Todd Jensen, Masterdramon and Thailog for keeping *Ask Greg* and the *Rain of the Ghosts* Wiki up and running.

Thanks to Jeffrey K., Julie Kane-Ritsch, Peter McHugh and Ellen Goldsmith-Vein for giving me and getting me the chance to write this. (And Sue helped too.) Nods also to Julie Nelson, Joey Villarreàl and everyone else at Gotham. And thanks to Michael Homler for giving me an annual kick-in-the-pants to keep at it.

Also at St. Martin's, Lisa Pompilio designed our lovely jacket; Sarah Jae-Jones held my hand through last-minute panic, and Elizabeth Catalano, Meryl Gross, Edwin Chapman, Joe Goldschein and Aleksandra Mencel all pitched in. It's appreciated.

Special thanks to Beth, Erin & Benny, Sheila & Wally, Robyn & Gwin, Jon & Dana, Jordan & Zelda, and Danielle & Brad, for their unending support.

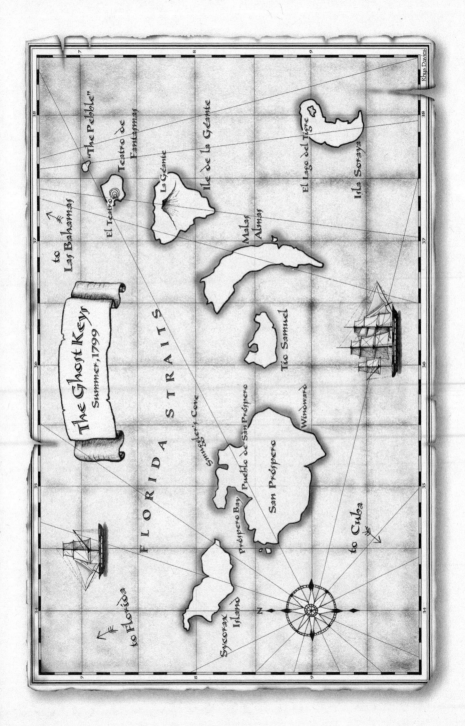

The Ghost Keys
Summer, 1799

FLORIDA STRAITS

to Las Bahamas

"The Pebble"

Teatro de Fantasmas

El Teatro

La Géante

Ile de la Géante

Malas Almas

El Lago del Tigre

Isla Soraya

Tío Samuel

Smuggler's Cove

Próspero Bay

Pueblo de San Próspero

San Próspero

Windward

Sycorax Island

to Florida

to Cuba

N

Rhys Davies

CHAPTER ONE

DRUMS

Rain could hear the drums as she raced past me. Of course, I knew there were no drums, but Rain usually had a soundtrack going nonstop in her head, and right now it was playing a major tribal beat. Or maybe that was just her pulse. She was pedaling like mad through the streets of San Próspero. Anxious but exhilarated. She didn't notice my companion or myself, but every other downbeat, she'd look back over her shoulder. *Were they behind her, ready to shoot? Would they be around the next corner? Or both?*

It was eight, nine o'clock at night on a Thursday. The moon hadn't risen yet, but San Próspero was a tourist town, a tourist island, so downtown was always well lit. A fine mist hung in the air, diffusing the light from the streetlamps, bathing everything in a soft glow. It was early September, hot and humid. It might rain any minute. Moisture, half condensation, half perspiration, beaded on Rain's copper skin, on her arms, legs and forehead. Her long dark hair, braided into a thick black rope, trailed behind her as she accelerated. Rain and Charlie were riding ten-speeds they had "rented" from Charlie's mom. (There hadn't been time to tell her about it.) Rain leaned in as her royal blue bike slid around a corner. Charlie followed suit on his gold one. He too looked over his shoulder. They had never been caught. But tonight the invaders seemed to be everywhere. I glanced toward Maq, but he was engrossed in the study of a mosquito that had lighted on his leathery arm. Clearly, he and I weren't going to intervene to help the kids.

Rain spotted another enemy contingent, coming down Brown's Road and heading straight for them. "Charlie! Evasive maneuvers! Veer off! Veer off!"

Together, and without hesitation or deceleration, they took the next corner, racing down a side street paved with cobblestones. The vibrations rattled up through their tires, playing out in Charlie's voice as he glanced over at her. "They control the whole island!"

Rain's face was a mask of intensity, but a sly smile crept into her eyes and then onto her mouth as the drums in her head pounded louder. "Never surrender!" she shouted back at him.

Charlie's dark brown eyes looked forward again. Two more at the other end of the street. He pointed ahead with one hand: "We're surrounded!" But Rain had already seen them and was pedaling even harder. Charlie matched speed, and their foes seemed to rush toward them. Then in perfect synch, the two teens turned down a dark alley, the bikes at a forty-five-degree angle.

The alley was practically an obstacle course. Charlie yelled out, "Dumpster at ten o'clock!"

"I see it!"

Dumpsters, wooden crates and other garbage made it impossible to ride abreast in the thin corridor between the two brick buildings. Rain pulled out in front. That was natural. She always took the lead. And Charlie always let her. He was very aware he always let her. He frowned slightly. They approached the mouth of the alley.

Rain called back over her shoulder, "We're almost out! Veer left!"

"No! They'll be waiting for us! Go right! Right!"

This time Rain's smile was obvious. She broke the alley and shot off to her left. Charlie shook his head ruefully, but he was hardly surprised. He followed her. Now they were on Camino de las Casas heading north toward the ocean. The street was packed with small shops on both sides, and there wouldn't be another place to turn off for half a mile. Charlie pulled up alongside, intent on reasoning with her at high speed. But it was too late. Both kids skidded to a harsh stop, a look of horror etched on their faces. The drums had instantly gone silent. They were caught. Trapped. And their attackers were preparing to shoot. "We're doomed," Charlie whispered.

Fortunately, the enemy—Bernie Cohen—was neither the swiftest nor the most coordinated of individuals. With his left hand, he fumbled for the outsized and outdated camera that hung around his neck against the background of his electric blue and gold Hawaiian shirt, while simultaneously pointing at Rain and Charlie with his right hand. The fact that he was right-handed made the whole camera manipulation thing that much more difficult. "Look, Maude," he said, "local color."

"Oh, they're perfect, Bernie. Get a picture."

"I am." But his right hand still hung in the air, and his wife's insistent elbow nudging only served to distract him further.

"Get a picture, Bernie," Maude kept saying. All this gave Charlie and Rain time to reevaluate the danger. Two tourists. Hefty and old. (Well, not really old. Bernie was only fifty-seven, and Maude was fifty-five. But to the two thirteen-year-olds, the Cohens seemed ancient.) Better yet, they were slow. There might still be time. Bernie now had a firm grip on the camera, but Rain and Charlie were already struggling to turn their bikes around.

It wasn't exactly a graceful endeavor. They were straddling the ten-speeds, and they were too close together. Charlie's pedal came very close to hooking the spokes of Rain's front wheel. "Hurry," she cried in a panic, "he's going to shoot!"

"I can see that!" (Really, Bernie & Maude and Charlie & Rain had much more in common than any of them realized.)

Once they had the bikes facing south, they hopped on the pedals and pushed off, fighting inertia. They had to get far enough fast enough so that Bernie wouldn't bother to shoot. Frankly, they wouldn't have made it if Maude hadn't given Bernie one last good elbow to the ribs, squealing, "Bernie, they're getting away!" Bernie had both hands on the camera and was taking aim, but he stopped to meet Maude's disapproving glare. By the time he rediscovered his viewfinder, the kids had disappeared into the mist.

I had left Maq to his bloodsucking friend. For reasons I still cannot explain, I felt a need to be there, to see even these events in person. I watched from the shadows as Bernie lowered his camera. His mind wasn't hard to read. *Drums,* he thought, *I think I hear drums.*

CHAPTER TWO

THE N.T.Z.

Rain knew Charlie was cross. She didn't have to glance over. She was sort of refusing to glance over. *Just wait for it,* she thought, and she kept pedaling.

Two seconds later, he said: "I *told* you to head right."

She knew he was right (correct), was usually right (correct). But she said, "Wouldn't have helped. There's only one safe place now. How long have we been out?"

Charlie looked down. His father's thick digital timepiece hung loosely on his wrist. It was in stopwatch mode. "Thirty-eight minutes. Not a record. But respectable."

"Forget the record. They're out in force tonight. And it doesn't help that you're wearing a T-shirt that says,

Local Color in big black letters. Let's head for cover while we can." And then, with all the melodrama she could muster, "To the N.T.Z.!" He nodded, and they both accelerated one more time.

Four and a half minutes later, they had reached the south end of the Camino where it abruptly met the San Próspero jungle. Immediately—and practically without slowing—they hopped off the bikes and stowed them out of sight among the dense ferns. Then—and again without slowing—Rain Cacique and Charlie Dauphin vanished into the green.

Or seemed to, anyway. There was no real path. But this island, this jungle, was their home. Thirteen years had taught them exactly where to go, how to move. They dodged branches and vines without thinking, stutter-stepped over roots, swung their hips around bushes, whirled past entire trees. More than anything, their progress resembled a kind of well-rehearsed free-style choreography, set to the fast tempo of the drums in their heads. The dance was quick and light; they left little trace behind, and their surroundings betrayed little movement, particularly in the light fog. Soon, the ground beneath their feet began to slope upward.

Charlie broke the silence first. He felt frustrated. Frustrated that they were almost caught. Frustrated that he always, always followed her lead. Even when he knew she was wrong. Even when *she* knew he was right. But *that* topic was too big to face, so: "Is it my imagination or is a simple game of *Attack of the Killer Tourists* getting harder and harder to win?"

She looked across at her lifelong best friend as they continued their uphill trek through the thick tangle. His big brown eyes met hers, and she wondered why she was always pushing things with him. It was all a jumble in her head. The tourists. Her parents. The tourists. The Ghosts. The tourists. The game. The tourists. Even Charlie. Maybe, it was because her life was entirely too mapped out. The mantra, *"Tourists own my future,"* played nearly as loud as the drums. There didn't seem to be any way around that. And for the first time it occurred to her that baiting Charlie was just a dopey attempt at rebelling against the inevitable. She risked his friendship, because she could. *I'm so stupid,* she thought. "Just keep moving," she said.

The unpath steepened, and the mist fell away. Seconds later, they reached THE SIGN, and they knew they were almost there. It was a PED X-ING sign that some long ago, nameless—but legendary—teen had stolen from downtown. Now it stood, incongruously planted in the middle of this dense growth of jungle. Its two iconically rendered pedestrians (one male, one female—and both tourists, of course) were surrounded by a crudely painted red circle with a red diagonal line running through them. Above the circle, the initials **N.T.Z.** were painted in big red letters.

The sight of it immediately brought smiles to their faces. The air seemed crisper; the weight of their "futures" seemed to vanish from their shoulders, and Rain was even briefly aware of the scent of wild vanilla orchids coming in lightly on a breeze. Without stopping, they plunged through a last dense stand of banana trees. "Go! Go!!" Rain yelled, as the drums reached their crescendo, and they BURST into the N.T.Z., arms raised in triumph!

The No Tourist Zone.

Synchronistically, a three-quarter moon slipped into the gap between two rain clouds to illuminate the clearing: a nearly perfect circle, some thirty feet in diameter, on the edge of a sheer cliff overlooking the Atlantic by at least a hundred feet. The rest of the N.T.Z. was surrounded by a virtual wall of wild banana plants and mahogany trees. If you didn't know where it was, you'd never find the place without a helicopter and a lot of patience.

Rain and Charlie rushed forward like long-distance runners who had just broken the tape at the finish line. They sidestepped the large central fire pit and stopped on the long block of sandstone at the cliff's edge. They smiled at each other. Rain's almond-shaped, almond-colored eyes sparkled as she said simply, "We made it." She threw her arms around him and gave him a joyous hug, instantly reminding Charlie why he let her get away with everything he let her get away with.

Partially, it was habit. But he was outgrowing that excuse. Mostly these days, it was this. This little rush that got his heart beating faster every time they got too close. For her, this hug was strictly platonic, like a hundred other platonic hugs they had shared since they were babies. But for him . . .

How did this happen?! When did this happen?! he wondered desperately. *Me and Rain? It's beyond nuts! Thank God she doesn't know!* And now came the worst part. The fracture in his brain between the side of him that needed the hug to end before she figured out his deep dark secret and the side that really kind of liked holding her and sort of wanted to stay this way forever.

And just then, an unfamiliar voice said, "Hi."

In unison, Rain and Charlie let out a little frightened yelp. Cheek to cheek, they turned as one—paralyzed in mid-embrace—to see a girl their age take a few cautious steps forward from the east edge of the clearing.

"I didn't mean to interrupt," she said, "but I figured you'd want to know you weren't alone."

Immediately, the embarrassed duo disengaged. Charlie

took a step back, "Hey, no biggie. We weren't doing *alone*."

But Rain was already advancing on the girl. "Hold on. How'd you find this place? It's a No Tourist Zone."

The girl took an involuntary step back. "I'm not a tourist," she said.

Rain looked her up and down. There weren't many local kids on San Próspero that Rain didn't know. There weren't any she hadn't met. It was just possible this girl was a local from one of the other Ghosts, La Géante maybe or Malas Almas, but she didn't look the part. She was shorter than Rain with large brown eyes and kewpie-doll lips that gave her a bit of a baby-face. Her wavy auburn hair was tied back into a loose pony that made her look even younger. But she was also more developed than Rain, which was a little annoying. She had light skin and the slightest hint of a Euro-Spanish accent hiding somewhere beneath her otherwise standard American English. But the big tip-off was what she was wearing. A sleeveless tee. A short summer skirt. Tennis shoes. Some kind of pendant around her neck. Small gold-hoop earrings. And all of it too chic, too new and too expensive. No one on Malas Almas could afford to dress like that. *Tourist*, Rain thought.

Charlie, meanwhile, had been checking out the stranger too. *She's cute*, he thought.

"Someone must have taken her up here," Rain said, loudly enough for the new girl to hear.

Charlie nodded absently, then was struck by a new and horrible thought: "Unless she followed us!"

"Oh, my God!" Rain said, panicked. *The unforgivable sin! We'll be banished! Excommunicated!*

The girl rushed a few steps forward to stem the tide. "I'm not a tourist," she repeated. "I was born here." She looked around. "Well, not here in the N.T.Z. But here. On the Prospero Keys."

Charlie groaned, now positive the girl was lying.

Rain spoke grimly, "Only tourists call these islands the *Prospero* Keys."

"The *Ghost* Keys. The Ghosts." The girl sounded a little desperate. Rain could almost see her mentally slapping herself over the error. "I've been away at boarding school. I had to call them the Prospero Keys there, or no one knew what I was talking about."

The girl stood as if waiting to be sentenced. Rain and Charlie exchanged looks. There was a long pause. Finally, Charlie shrugged: "She must be legit. There's no way a local would reveal the N.T.Z. to a stranger."

Rain averted her eyes, kicked the ground and mumbled, "What if she *did* follow us?"

"Don't even go there," Charlie said flatly.

"I didn't follow you. Honest." She took another

tentative step. "It took me awhile, but I found the place from memory."

Charlie made a conscious decision to relax. Better to believe her than to accept the alternative—and the consequences. He approached her, saying, "I'm Charlie Dauphin. This is Rain Cacique. Welcome home."

The girl breathed an audible sigh of relief. "Thanks. My name's Miranda Guerrero." She and Charlie met beside the dormant fire pit. For a second she thought that maybe he might want to shake hands or something, but he just shoved his fists into the front pockets of his shorts. She didn't know what to do with her own hands. They seemed to be on the verge of flailing about, so she clasped them together behind her back. She felt like a complete dork. Like a tourist. But he smiled at her, which was nice. She spoke to the smile. "It's nice to meet someone my age, you know, with school starting Monday—"

Rain groaned. "Don't remind me."

"Sorry, sorry, it's just . . ." Miranda trailed off, looking stricken. She glanced nervously toward Rain, afraid that she'd struck another sore spot with the girl. The boy seemed friendly enough. He had cocoa-brown skin and a short black Afro, a wide face, open and kind, with big dark eyes, and an easygoing manner. But the girl. The girl was imposing. As tall as the boy. Copper skin, long black hair and light brown eyes that seemed to look right through you. She seemed very aggressive, and Miranda was sure she had blown it with her.

Oh, just go for it, she thought. *Nothing to lose now.* "Do you guys want to go waterskiing tomorrow on my dad's boat?"

Rain and Charlie rolled their eyes dismissively. To Miranda, it almost seemed like a move they had practiced for timing. Charlie shook his head, and Miranda bit her lip and looked away. Then Rain spoke.

CHAPTER THREE

SNAKES

Charlie was still shaking his head. "I can't believe you said yes." He and Rain were walking the two bikes into his mom's gated lockup. There was a sign over their heads: ROYAL DOLPHIN RENTALS— BICYCLES, MOPEDS, CANOES. A gray-blue plywood dolphin with a big grin and a golden crown leapt above the words and the rows and rows of bicycles and tandem bikes and bikes that pulled car seats on wheels and giant tricycles with giant baskets and mopeds and neat stacks of canoes and kayaks and surfboards. There were even three Jet Skis and two Jeeps.

Rain leaned back against the fence as Charlie knelt down to lock the borrowed bikes to their racks. "Why wouldn't I say yes?" she asked.

"After the way you interrogated her?"

"Waterskiing, Charlie. It was a good offer. Besides, if we weren't a little shallow, we wouldn't be teenagers." On cue, Ramon Hernandez cruised by in a beat-up convertible jam-packed with teens. Metal blared from tinny speakers. Laughter and shouting from about eight mouths. Marina Cortez—a tall dark-haired girl who was sitting up on the chassis with her feet down on the backseat—was the only one to even glance toward Rain, before quickly turning away. Rain didn't feel snubbed, exactly. It was simply the order of things. She and Charlie were about to start eighth grade. High school seniors were not programmed to give them the time of day. Ramon's convertible, a tremendous symbol of freedom despite its dragging rear bumper, turned a corner. Rain's gaze lingered wistfully on its absence. Then she looked around the lockup. "Next time, I think we should rent mopeds."

Charlie stood up. "Mom'll love that."

Rain smiled and shrugged.

Charlie stared at the mopeds. "Of course, we do need to cram in the fun before school starts—"

"And life ends."

"And life ends." He led Rain out and locked the gates behind them. The mist, by this time, had descended in force.

Rain spoke, casually doomed. "Three more days. The horror. The horror."

Charlie looked at Rain. At first her eyes focused on him, smiling. Her eyes always smiled more than her mouth. But gradually they began to lose focus. Or rather, they focused on something he couldn't see. On something inside her that made her feel sad and small and trapped. When she spoke again, it was barely a whisper: "I better get home."

"Uh, sure. I'll see ya."

She was already walking backward down the street. She waved to him. "Bye." And turned around, jamming her hands into the pockets of her shorts. He watched her until she turned the corner. Then he walked the half block past the lockup to his house and the chewing out he knew his mom was going to give him for taking the bikes without permission.

By this time, the drums in Rain's head had quieted, replaced by a sort of slinky piano that kind of gave her the creeps. It was late as she passed from the shoreline neighborhood where the Dauphins lived and into Old Town. Most tourists stayed downtown or by the beach, so Old Town's "charming" cobblestone streets were not nearly as well lit. It began to drizzle. Rain felt a few drops and then the cold icky of a big drip on her scalp.

Pausing beneath a lone wrought-iron streetlamp, she looked up toward the heavens and said, "Terrific."

She started out again, picking up speed as it began to rain in earnest. Her sneakers barely made a sound on the cobbles, so it startled her when she realized she could hear footsteps. Heavy footsteps. Clomping on the cobblestones. She didn't stop, but she looked behind her, back down the dark lane. She didn't see anyone. But the footsteps kept coming, slow and steady. She mentally reprimanded herself. She knew that sound carried forever in the fog on these stone streets. Her father had told her as much on another scary night— *when she was six!* The sound of the footsteps was probably coming from three blocks over or from someone heading in the opposite direction or both. She passed under another solitary streetlamp and felt a bit better.

But if anything, the footsteps were getting louder. Their pace increasing. She glanced back over her shoulder and saw a shadow pass quickly under the lamplight. A big shadow.

Rain didn't want to run. She was afraid to run. Afraid that acknowledging the danger would make it real. But as she turned down Rue de Lafitte, her own speed increased involuntarily.

The rain was coming down even harder now. Maybe

she *could* run. Just to avoid getting soaked. She looked back again. The shadowy figure had turned the corner. The distance between them was decreasing.

She ran. Turned onto Goodfellow Lane, simultaneous with a silent flash of lightning that heralded a real downpour. In response, the heavy boots of the shadowed man started to run as well, clomping and splashing on the wet stones, gaining on her. She beelined for the only streetlamp on the block.

She stopped beneath it, needing the light. He was close now. Just beyond the light, the footsteps slowed and stopped. A rumble of thunder jolted her into action. She wheeled on the shadow and yelled defiantly: "Take another step, and I'll cut you off at the knees!" Her bravado ebbed pathetically. "Or . . . I'll scream. My parents are right inside."

She still couldn't see her pursuer clearly. Just a shadow. A very big shadow. Ignoring her warning, it took one deliberate step toward her into the light—which hardly made it any less menacing. The streetlamp revealed a big man, considerably over six feet. He had tanned weathered skin, a spiky blond crewcut and ice blue eyes that accented a permanent scowl. Water dripped down the side of his face. He ignored that too.

She couldn't move or make a sound. He looked down on her like she was a bug to be squashed under those clomping boots. Finally, he spoke: "Wasn't following you, kid." He had an Australian accent.

He nodded his head to the left, toward the three-story building illuminated by the streetlight. Rain glanced quickly at the sign—THE NITAINO INN—as the man continued, "Got a reservation at the Inn here."

Rain squeaked out, "You ran after me."

"Just trying to get out of the rain." He sneered at her. "Still trying." Rain just stared at him. He held up a duffel bag as if to prove he had luggage and was therefore on the level.

It worked. Immediately, Rain felt mortified. He was a tourist. "Uh, okay then," she said. "Right this way." She quickly ran up the four steps to the front door of the Inn and opened it. He followed.

The lobby of the Nitaino Inn was painted in warm island colors. It was presently deserted, and as she and the man shook the rainwater off, Rain called out, "Mom! We've got a guest!"

Almost magically, Rain's mother appeared on the landing above them and quickly but gracefully descended the stairs. "Rain, I'm right here." Translation: *Don't shout!*

"Sorry." Still a bit freaked, Rain put some distance between herself and the stranger. She slid past the front desk and hesitated at the door to the darkened dining room. She forced herself to meet that cold blue gaze. "And sorry about the mix-up."

"I'll try to survive the shame."

Rain's mom raised an eyebrow in Rain's direction as she stepped behind the front desk. She opened the register and turned it to face her new guest. "My name's Iris Cacique. Welcome to the Nitaino Inn, Mister . . ."

He picked up a pen and glanced down at the book. Currently, there were five other guests listed:

Rebecca Sawyer, Hannibal, MO
Mr. & Mrs. John DeLancy, San Francisco
Terry Chung and Elizabeth Ellis-Chung, Cambridge, Mass.

The stranger wrote only one word.

"Callahan," he said. "Name's Callahan."

Rain gave him one last look and retreated out of the lobby.

The Nitaino Inn was a Bed & Breakfast with a good reputation in the guidebooks. Rain lived there with her parents and grandfather and whatever tourists happened to be staying in the Inn's six guest rooms. They were rarely full (outside the High Season). Old Town was a popular tourist attraction—during the day. Antique shops, galleries, craftsmen with pushcarts and those oh-so-charming cobblestone streets brought a nice walk-through business in good weather. But parking was problematic, and it was a fair distance to the water. And no fast food or chain stores at all. People walked through Old Town, but they tended not to sleep there. Still, Iris ran a tight, clean ship and served large portions of good food every morning, so although they were rarely full, they were also rarely vacant. Rain had grown up that way. In a house she shared with both family and strangers. Privacy, real privacy, was something she had read about in books. As she passed through the dining room, she wasn't surprised to see a light on in the kitchen. All she could do was hope it was her father and not a tourist "just grabbing a quick bite."

She pushed open the swinging door. A man with long gray hair sat at the kitchen table with his back to her. Immediately, she relaxed. Not a tourist. Not even her dad. Better. "Hey, 'Bastian," she said, smiling for the first time since she left Charlie at the lockup.

"Hi, Raindrop."

Sebastian Bohique was Rain's maternal grandfather and just about her favorite person on the planet. He was a month shy of ninety years old but was sitting there eating a very sugary breakfast cereal, the one that came in the shape of hearts, moons, stars, clovers and new blue whales. Rain crossed to the cupboard, opened the wood and glass door and pulled out a bowl. She glanced out the window. It was still pouring. A flash of lightning was followed seconds later by a crack of thunder. The storm-head was getting closer.

"Rain." Her father's voice. She turned toward the doorway to the laundry room. Alonso Cacique stood there with a basketful of white towels. "I've got a charter tomorrow. I'll need you to work the boat with me."

Rain's expression, not to mention her posture, took a nosedive. She threw out her arms (bowl and all). "Dad, I can't! I've got plans with Charlie."

"You see Charlie every day."

"We're going waterskiing! We just got invited tonight!"

"And the charter came in this afternoon." He approached her. Calm but firm. "You should have checked with me first."

Papa 'Bastian looked up from his cereal. "I'll cover for her, Alonso."

"That's not your job, 'Bastian."

'Bastian shrugged. "I know. But school starts Monday. Let's cut her some slack."

Rain became a sudden and exaggerated supplicant. "Yes. Slack. Pleeeassse!"

Alonso shook his head, but his eyes were smiling. "All right. Just this once."

Rain leaned over the laundry basket and gave her dad a peck on the cheek. "Thanks, Dad."

By now, Alonso was smiling with his mouth as well. "Thank your grandfather."

"I will."

Still smiling and shaking his head, Alonso did a quick about-face and headed back out the door. Rain stood there, staring at nothing in particular. 'Bastian snuck a glance at her. She looked down at the cereal bowl in her hand as if it were a strange artifact from another world. Then she placed it absently on the counter and sighed deeply.

"Well, I'm waiting," 'Bastian said.

Rain's head turned slowly toward him. "What for?"

'Bastian gave her his patented Old Man Twinkle. "My thank-you."

Rain walked around the table, pulled an empty chair out of the way and kissed him on the forehead. "Sorry. Thanks. You saved me." She looked down at the empty chair and thought about sitting down. The simplest decision suddenly seemed very hard to make. Or so unimportant that it was impossible to care.

"So how come you're not happy?"

Rain collapsed into the chair. "I'm thirteen years old, and my life is *over!*" she moaned.

It seemed to 'Bastian that she was auditioning to be

the poster child for teen angst and melodramatic defeat. He nodded solemnly. "I see. And how did you come by this revelation . . . ?"

"*Summer's over!* I can't pretend anymore. I'm trapped, Papa. Totally trapped."

Papa Sebastian leaned his head away, scratching one eyebrow with his pinky so that he wouldn't have to meet her gaze. "That's a problem, all right."

But she wasn't fooled. She gave him a gentle punch on the shoulder. "Don't laugh," she said. "You don't know what it's like. You've been places. To the mainland, to Europe."

His whole body tensed up; he responded in clipped tones. "I wasn't exactly on holiday, young lady."

"That's the point. You did something important with your life. I'm never going to *do* anything. I'll never *go* anywhere. I'll graduate high school and spend the rest of my life ushering tourists around these same eight islands!" She slumped down dramatically, like a puppet whose strings have been cut, her head buried in her hands on the table.

Sebastian quickly pushed away an old memory and eyed her wryly. He paused just long enough for her to be sure that he'd received the full effect of her performance. Then he spoke quietly. "Now I don't believe that, Raindrop. I don't believe that for a second."

She didn't budge, but he knew she was listening, so he continued: "This is home. And frankly, it's not a bad place to make a life. So you may come back someday to usher tourists." He shrugged. "After all, I did. But you'll get your own chance to decide."

Still no movement. "You've always been special, Rain. An adventurer. We'd turn our backs for a minute, and you'd be off exploring. Before you could walk, even. And I remember watching you as you grew up. You'd have long conversations with your imaginary friends. You'd fight pirates. Find treasure. Solve mysteries. I knew you were destined for greatness."

She refused to lift her head. But at least she spoke—a sarcastic "Right."

Sebastian placed a gentle hand on Rain's head. His gold wristband caught the flash from another burst of lightning and sparkled. "It's like my *abuela* used to say . . . *'To unlock a door, you need two things: a key and someone who knows how to turn it.'*"

Rain's arms and the thunder muffled her reply. "I never knew what that meant. And what does it have to do with anything, anyway?"

He leaned down to whisper in her ear, "You strike me as someone who knows how to turn a key."

Sebastian leaned back again, and slowly, tentatively, as if he had been working magic upon her, Rain started to raise her head to meet his warm gray eyes. "Maybe," she said begrudgingly. "But I'm never gonna get my hands on any key. Not to anyplace I'd want to go."

Papa Sebastian considered this for a moment. Rain watched him stare down at the milk in his cereal bowl. Outside, the wind howled, and another lightning bolt lit up the windows. The thunder was nearly simultaneous; the storm was right over their heads. In contrast to that fury, the music in her head, which had been silent since she had yelled at Callahan out on the street, played a slow and pretty jazz cornet. Something was going to happen. Abruptly, he pushed the bowl away. "Let's start here," he said. He removed the gold band from around his right wrist. "I've been meaning to give you this for a while."

He held it out to her on the palm of his hand: two gold snakes intertwined, braided almost, clasping each other's tails in their mouths. Again, the band caught the light. She knew what this meant to him and shook her head. "'Bastian . . . Your grandmother gave you that."

"That's right. Been in the family for four hundred years." One of the snakes had two tiny chips of blue stone for eyes. Rain looked from those eyes into 'Bastian's. His were smiling, and her own started to smile as well. "Always made me feel like I was part of something larger than myself," he said. "A span of generations and traditions."

Rain's eyes widened. She knew this was a big moment, even if she didn't quite know why. Maybe for just that reason, she resisted. "It's not exactly my ticket out of here."

But Sebastian would not be swayed. He took hold of her left arm. The thunder growled at them both. "It's yours now," he said. Rain swallowed hard as he slipped the band onto her slim wrist. It was too big for her. 'Bastian paused for a moment, tilting his head to consider the problem or maybe just to listen to the storm. Then he slid it up around her biceps, until it was snug. A perfect fit. "You can wear it up here. That'll look hip."

"Yeah," she said, smiling and unconcerned with how it looked. She felt immensely grateful to the old man; he had a knack for making her feel special, for making her limited world seem limitless. Her eyes were focused on his, so she hardly noticed when he let go of the gold band. If she had, she might have also noticed the blue snake eyes *flash* for an instant. A mere trick of the light, perhaps, amid multiple lightning strikes and angry thunder.

His thoughts were focused inward. His heart was full of familial pride, but he also felt suddenly weary. So he was distracted and didn't notice the other snake, the eyeless snake, momentarily glowing—nor the same soft golden light shining briefly within his granddaughter's brown eyes.

Rain felt dizzy. She lowered her head, let out a little moan, and for a second her body reeled; she almost tipped right out of her chair. Sebastian regained focus and reached out to steady her with his hand. "Raindrop, kiddo, you okay?"

"I'm fine," she said and meant it. She raised her eyes again and almost took his breath away. Of course, he always thought his granddaughter was pretty. He was biased; he'd admit it. *But now she looks positively radiant.* He was reminded of his late wife, Iris' mother. A woman who spent her whole life almost mystically at peace with the world.

He kept his hand on her shoulder. She placed hers on his. "Really, Papa. I feel good. Thanks."

"*You* . . . are welcome." Then, with a grunt, he hoisted himself up onto his feet. The old wound was really killing him tonight. "Just put the milk away, okay? I'm beat."

"Sure, Papa." As he limped out the door, she gathered up the milk carton, the cereal box and his bowl. Another bolt of lightning flashed outside. The thunder came a full second later. The storm seemed to be moving on.

She listened to 'Bastian's footsteps as he slowly

climbed the back stairs to his third-floor room. Then she rinsed out the bowl and spoon. Put away the milk, the cereal and her own unused bowl. She crossed back through the dining room and into the lobby.

Her father was there, checking in yet another late arrival. This one was a very tall woman with long black hair. She smiled at Rain. Red lips and dark eyes. Rain smiled back politely and headed up the front stairs.

Rain's room was on the second floor. First door on the left, facing Goodfellow Lane. As she reached the top of the stairs, her mother came out of the guest room across the hall. "We serve breakfast from seven to ten."

Callahan filled the doorway. His eyes looked past Iris to Rain, who glanced over her shoulder at him, before pulling out her key and unlocking her room. Iris didn't notice. She was in hostess mode. "Please let me know if there's anything I can do to make your stay a pleasant one."

Callahan's brow furrowed. "Get back to you on that," he said.

Rain shuddered involuntarily. Iris didn't see it but somehow sensed it and turned toward her daughter. Rain smiled, shrugged at her mother and entered her room, closing—and locking—the door behind her. There was no doubt about it. This Callahan guy gave her the creeps in a major way.

But he didn't occupy her mind for long. She paused in front of the dresser mirror to admire her new armband. She had to admit it did look pretty cool around her biceps. "I'm hip," she said aloud. She giggled. Then she carefully removed it from her arm and placed it on the nightstand. It was late, and she was going waterskiing in the morning. She quickly got ready for bed and turned out the light.

Soon the steady beat of the rain had lulled her to sleep. Outside, Maq and I stood vigil in the downpour, all through the night.

CHAPTER FOUR

THE GHOSTS

Somewhere along the line, I'd been dubbed "Opie." It wasn't my real name, of course, but I'd gotten used to it, and at any rate I wasn't one to complain. I spent most of my time with an old beach bum that the locals knew as "Maq" (though that wasn't *his* true name either). I was Maq's best friend, and he was mine. We disagreed sometimes, but considering we were never too sure where our next meal was coming from, we got along just fine.

Maq and I know things.

Lately, he's grown a bit scattered, but Maq can see into the future. No joke. He knew we'd find lunch behind the Versailles Hotel, and that night he had us standing outside the Nitaino for Rain's reawakening before she even got to the kitchen. When the snake's golden glow lit up her eyes, we could both feel it from the street—and despite the weather, it warmed us to our bones.

I couldn't see the future. I could guess at it like anyone. And I had a more-than-decent memory for the past. But my real talent was the present. I knew what was happening—wherever it was happening—now. I knew what was being done. I knew what was being said. I even knew what was being thought. It came in handy, given my line of work, but it's not nearly as much fun as it sounds.

Still, that's why Maq and I made such a great team. We complemented each other. I handled the here and now; he handled the yet to come. Had to be that way. He was (to say the least) a bit vague on the present.

At present, Rain was dreaming. All through the night, she had slept the sleep of the dead. But just before sunrise, rapidly behind closed lids, her eyes began to track back and forth in her skull. She was alone on cobblestone streets. Surrounded by shadows seeking to hem her in. She ran, breathing hard, frightened. Bernie Cohen blocked her course. She tried to slip past, but his garish shirt seemed to swell up to fill the lane, and his increasing bulk forced her away. She stumbled backward, turned, tripped, fell to her knees. Tourists loomed above her. Bernie Cohen, Maude Cohen, Rebecca Sawyer and the shadows of a hundred others she had served breakfast to at the Inn, had carried bait for on the boat.

'Bastian called out to her. Her parents, too. She could barely get her legs and arms to move; she crawled as if through Sycorax Honey, desperate to reach her family. 'Bastian pointed. The armband lay on the ground before her, shining gold. *The Key!* Just out of reach. She struggled forward, aware she was being pursued. She glanced back over her shoulder. *Callahan!* Gaining on her with every lightning strike. Gaining; he would catch her. She found her hand grasping the armband. She turned to look. The two golden snakes were wrapped around her biceps. They had come to life, growing, binding, constricting her entire body. The blue-eyed serpent opened wide its black maw, threatening to swallow her whole. She screamed silently at her parents . . . wordlessly begged her grandfather for help . . . but they simply nodded their approval. . . . Darkness.

And then the smallest fragment of light. Glowing white like a frosted Christmas bulb behind her. She turned to find a hand reaching to pull her out. She lunged for it; she couldn't reach; she couldn't reach. *I can't reach you!* She caught hold. The hand pulled her from the darkness into the frosty light. Into winter snow. *I've never seen snow!* She was in a city. A big city frosted with beautiful lights and snow, black and white, like old movies. It was wonderful. She was so grateful. So grateful. But who had pulled her out? She turned. A woman. A very tall woman with dark hair, dark eyes and a kind smile. She knew this woman. From somewhere. Somewhere.

"You don't belong back there," the woman said gently. "Leave it all behind."

Rain nodded. *That's right. That's right.*

"You have the whole world to explore," the woman said warmly. "There's so much to see."

Rain could only nod. So grateful. So much to see. She wandered forward. The snow was white and warm and glowed softly, quietly. *So much to see.*

She turned a corner to find Charlie waiting. He cocked his head. "What took you so long?"

She shrugged. So much to see. The snow melted away, leaving a big world in bright warm hues. Tall purple skyscrapers. A bright orange calliope. A red carousel with every horse in the rainbow. Her best friend beside her. And so much to see. *This is where I belong. I don't want to go back.*

But in her bedroom—in her bed—she began to stir. Something nagged at her, something that seemed to pull her out of this pleasant dream, this vision of her and Charlie walking through a color-drenched cartoon of New York City. Funhouse music, new surroundings, the arrival of Daffy Duck—none of it could hold her.

There was a man in her room.

She was aware of him watching before she had even opened her eyes. The dream faded to black. Charlie and Daffy disappeared. She caught one last glimpse of the beautiful Tall Woman, and then she was alone with the intruder. He was reaching for her. She tried to pull away but could barely manage a cringe. Did his hand graze her skin? She felt nothing tangible—just a chill that wracked her body like a spasm. She tried to speak, but it took all her strength to move her lips, and no sound came out. Finally, she forced her eyes open. The room was still dark. But he was still there. Looming over her bed. Reaching for her again. Black hair. Broad shoulders. She managed to shrink back against her headboard.

This time she *made* herself speak, each syllable a massive effort, almost painful. "Who—are—you?"

Dawn came. Rays of morning sunlight streamed in through her window. For just a second, she squeezed her eyes shut against the sudden glare. She reopened them immediately and thought she caught a glimpse of his silhouette moving fast toward her nightstand. Her head turned to follow the movement, but he wasn't there. Just her grandfather's armband, cheerfully reflecting the sun. She scanned the room. Rubbed her eyes. Looked again. There was no man. Awake now in a light-filled space, there was no man. Breathing hard, she leapt to her feet. Stood there in her pajamas, unsure. Then she checked the door. Locked. The windows. Locked. Under the bed. Nothing. With dread, she opened the closet. Jammed with stuff but no bodies. With greater dread now, the bathroom. No one hiding in the shower. And behind the door . . . absolutely no one.

It had all been a dream. And the dark man, just a remnant of that dream. The ghost of a remnant. She looked at the clock. A good two hours remained before she needed to leave the Inn. She sighed and started her day. She'd shower when she got back from the water, but she washed her face and brushed her teeth without ever letting her eyes stray from the mirror. No ghosts were going to sneak up on Rain Cacique. She brushed her long hair and braided it into the thick rope she favored. Got dressed. She paused over 'Bastian's armband. If she lost it on the water, she'd never forgive herself. *And besides . . .*

She left it on the nightstand and went downstairs. As she walked through the lobby, she remembered the Tall

Woman who had checked in the night before. On a whim, she checked the guest register:

Rebecca Sawyer, Hannibal, MO
Mr. & Mrs. John DeLancy, San Francisco
Terry Chung and Elizabeth Ellis-Chung, Cambridge, Mass.
Callahan
Judith Vendaval, New York.

The Tall Woman was from New York. The dream was already fading away, but Rain still recalled the friendly smile and the wintry streets of the city. Had Rain seen Ms. Vendaval sign the book the night before or had she guessed the woman's home from her sophisticated clothes or was it all just a big coincidence? She shrugged it off and closed the book. Maybe she'd see the lady at breakfast.

Her mother was already up and cooking. Rain helped serve the guests. Neither Ms. Vendaval nor Callahan (nor any dark ghost) came down to eat, but the DeLancys were demanding enough that she didn't miss the extra work. As it was, Rain still had to wash the dishes, fold some towels in the laundry room and beg Iris to make the beds for her. By the time she met Charlie at the docks, she had all but forgotten how her morning had begun.

Miranda was waiting at the gate to the Columbia Yacht Club. She seemed immediately relieved to see them, as if she hadn't been sure they were going to show up.

"I wasn't sure you were going to show up," she said. Rain looked at Charlie and rolled her eyes. He elbowed her to lay off.

Miranda led them down a gangway to a sleek thirty-foot twin-engine speedboat. It was brand-new, and Rain figured it was worth about ten times her dad's charter. A woman in her late twenties with short blond hair and tan skin held out her hand to help Miranda board. Rain and Charlie followed. As an afterthought, Miranda said, "Oh, this is Ariel." Rain and Charlie both said hi. But the woman only nodded silently and untied the line. She took the helm and piloted the boat smoothly out onto the water beyond Pueblo Harbor.

On most any map, they were labeled the Prospero Keys: a chain of tropical islands on the edge of the Bermuda Triangle—southeast of Florida, midway between the Bahamas and Cuba. Locals, however, never referred to the Prosperos by their official name. To the native born, they were the Ghost Keys, or simply, "The Ghosts."

The Keys were an American Territory. The main industry was tourism, but there were also substantial fishing and agricultural interests, a U.S. military base and burgeoning industrial growth. The capital city,

Pueblo de San Próspero (where Rain and Charlie were both born and raised), was a medium-sized destination resort. Tourist trade made it seem bigger than it really was. For full-time residents, the Pueblo was really just a small town on the edge of the jungle where everybody knew everybody else's name, business and secrets.

There were eight islands. San Próspero was the largest. Sycorax Island was a ferry ride to the west. Five others arced to the northeast in a gentle curve: Tío Samuel, Malas Almas, Ile de la Géante, Teatro de Fantasmas and a strip of sand that locals called "The Pebble." The eighth island, Isla Soraya, was some small distance south of the other seven.

Miranda's father's boat took the kids beyond the already crowded Próspero Bay and into the Florida Straits. Ariel cut the engine and immediately began helping the three teens get prepped. Charlie and Miranda were gamely trying to generate some small talk between them. But Rain watched Ariel. There was something strangely compelling about the woman. It wasn't simply that she was beautiful. It was the way she went about her business. There was a precision, an economy of movement. There was nothing loose about her. She never spoke; in fact, she might have been mute for all Rain knew. She seemed somehow coiled and ready to spring.

Miranda still felt nervous around Rain, as if Rain

had put her on some kind of probation, which wasn't exactly an inaccurate assessment. Trying to gain some points, Miranda asked her new companion if she wanted to go first. Rain jumped at the chance, and a few minutes later she was out on the water, wind and spray in her face. An electric guitar was rockin' out fifties-style in her head as she rode the single wide ski and called out for Ariel to open her up. Ariel complied, and Rain's smile broadened with the increased velocity. All thoughts of school and tourists and unfulfilled dreams were forgotten. She was in the moment. She was free.

Back on the boat, Charlie and Miranda watched as Rain began sliding her ski back and forth across the boat's wake, getting a little bit of air with each pass. Miranda was impressed. "Wow. She's great."

"Yeah," Charlie said dreamily. He was in major crush mode, and Miranda immediately picked up on it and turned to look at him. Charlie caught the look and snapped himself out of it. "I mean her skiing."

Miranda nodded. She was mildly disappointed. The hug she had caught them in the night before had been a tip-off, but Charlie was really nice, and she had thought maybe . . . Still, it was good to know. These were her first friends since moving home. She definitely didn't want to come between them. She did wonder if Rain felt the same way about Charlie, or even if she knew how he felt. It didn't seem like they were a real couple.

Meanwhile, Charlie was babbling. "See, this is her routine. She's got it down to a science. Wake-jumping. And look, left hand in the air. She's gonna do a turn-around." On cue, Rain, holding on with just her right hand, executed a sweet three-sixty on her ski. For a split-second, she released the line completely then grabbed for it again with her left hand.

And missed! Instantly, she started to lose it. A look of panic swept over her face as she wiped out big-time.

Charlie shouted, "Rain!"

And Miranda: "Stop! Stop the boat!" Ariel was already decelerating and bringing it around. She had the speedboat dead in the water within five seconds, but they had already lost sight of Rain. Charlie was ready to dive in—in fact they all were—when Rain's ski abruptly popped up to the surface without her. Charlie froze. Exactly three more seconds passed.

Rain surfaced, sputtering. Fine, but embarrassed, she treaded water and waved sheepishly. Ariel pulled the boat alongside, and Rain climbed aboard. Charlie glared. Rain shrugged. "Whoops."

Charlie took his turn skiing. Then Miranda. Rain again. Charlie. Miranda. As Charlie helped Miranda back aboard, Rain offered to take the boat and let Ariel go next. Ariel looked at her. Then she shook her head; it was a tiny back and forth movement, just exactly what was necessary to convey the message "no." *Maybe she is mute,* Rain thought.

They headed back to the bay, to the harbor. Ariel at the helm. The three kids stood on the deck, enjoying the sun and the salt air. Rain toweled off, then suddenly turned to Charlie. "Oh, I had the weirdest dream this morning."

"Yeah?"

"Yeah. You were in it. And this woman—a new guest at the Inn. I don't remember exactly. I think we were all in New York City."

"What would you know about New York City?"

"I watch television. Duh. Anyway, the dream changed, and I was back in my room. There was a man standing over me. It felt so real, I jumped out of bed."

"That's creepy," Charlie said. He glanced over Rain's shoulder at Miranda. Rain had virtually turned her back on the new girl, and Miranda was clearly feeling unincluded and borderline lonely. She took a step away.

"I searched the entire room," Rain was saying. Charlie tapped her knee with one hand and nodded toward Miranda. Rain turned. "Hmm?"

She took another look at the girl. As much as Rain wanted to leave the Ghosts, it must be even tougher to come back here to stay. The place was so insular. Rain and Charlie were so insular. So self-sufficient. A wave of empathy washed over Rain. "Miranda?" she said. Miranda turned toward her.

"*¿Hablas español?*" Rain asked.

"Hey, wait!" Charlie sputtered. This was backfiring.

Miranda's eyes ping-ponged between them. Cautiously, she said, "*Sí. Por supuesto.*"

Charlie shook his head, mock furious. "I seem to recall that English is the official language of the Ghost Keys."

Rain ignored him and leaned toward Miranda conspiratorially. "*Que bueno. Porque Charlie no habla y esto le vuelve loco.*"

Charlie recognized the word *loco*, knew Rain was trying to drive him crazy and bellowed, "*Enough!*" at the top of his lungs. The girls laughed. Charlie shook his head. But he saw how Miranda was smiling. How Rain had finally opened up and let her in. It was a good thing, even if it had been at his expense. Soon he was smiling too.

"Thanks, you guys," Miranda said. "I mean, thanks for coming today."

Charlie shrugged, "Free boat, good weather."

And Rain, "You did make it hard." They all laughed again.

Maq was down on the beach, bumming French fries off the tourists, but I wanted to see this in person, so I was watching from about twenty yards down the dock when Ariel eased the boat into its slip. The kids all jumped down as one to tie it off. Rain was saying, "You know the End of Summer Party is Sunday night at the N.T.Z. . . . unless it rains."

Charlie piped in, "Yeah, Miranda, you should meet us there . . . unless it rains."

Miranda positively beamed. "Thanks. I think I will . . . unless it rains." It was all very sweet and nice to see, but that wasn't why I had come.

Another voice, an adult voice, said, "Rain."

Rain was still smiling when she turned toward her father. But the smile quickly froze. The guitars in her head went silent. Alonso Cacique was standing on the dock, standing as if he had been waiting there for some time. He lowered his head sadly.

"Dad . . . ?"

Charlie and Miranda straightened up. Ariel's head turned half an inch.

Rain walked toward her father. "What is it? What's wrong?" He put his arm around her and whispered something too low for the rest of us to hear. Immediately, Rain began to cry, softly, as if somewhere deep inside her she had already known (and what Alonso had said was mere confirmation). Miranda and Charlie exchanged a concerned glance. They didn't have any idea what to do, what was wrong or how to comfort their friend. I had considerably more information, but I felt guilty being there. An intruder. Maq had been right to stay away. This wasn't our business really. Not this part. The saving grace was that they hadn't seen me yet. I spun around and trotted off toward the beach. Maq'd have a sympathetic smile for me and maybe even a hot dog. And he almost never said, "I told you so." It was one of his finer, less human, qualities.

CHAPTER FIVE

SUNSET

Alonso brought his daughter home, double-parking his battered jeep in front of the Inn. He stared straight ahead and inhaled deeply. This was hard for him too. He knew he had to stay strong for Iris and for Rain, but it was very hard for him too. He said, "I need to find a place to park. Do you want to—"

Rain jumped out of the car before he could finish. She ran wildly up the four steps and practically crashed her way through the front door and inside. In similar fashion, she raced up the stairs. Tears had given way to sobs, and she was having trouble catching her breath. At the head of the stairs, she froze. The smallest gasp escaped her lips.

Callahan, the world's scariest tourist, was standing

51

with his hand on the knob of *her* bedroom door. Going in? Coming out? It wasn't clear. He saw her there, and fumfered out: "Wait. Ain't my room. Got turned around."

Silent, sad and angry, Rain approached her door as Callahan crossed the hall to his. He quickly opened it. It was unlocked. "Right," he said. "This is it."

Then he paused. Turned back toward her. His scowling expression didn't change, but he said, "Heard about your grandfather. Sorry." Then without waiting for a response, he entered his guest room and shut the door behind him. Rain found herself staring at that closed door. She shook her head, shook him off *in* her head and unlocked her room.

She swung the door open but stood there paralyzed for what seemed the longest time. The room was a prison she was voluntarily entering to serve out an endless sentence. Without him.

Without him, she surrendered. She broke into tears again and flung herself onto the bed. Giant sobs wracked her young body.

"Rain? Honey?" Iris stood in the open doorway. She'd been crying too. She crossed the room and sat down.

Rain quickly sat up and threw her arms around her mother. "Oh, Mom, I can't believe he's gone."

Iris wrapped her arms around Rain and gently stroked her daughter's hair. "Neither can I. He seemed so endless. But it was peaceful. In his sleep. He didn't suffer."

"But he . . . It's just . . . Talking to him . . ."

"I know. The world seemed full of possibilities."

Rain buried her head in her mother's breast. Both of them were crying now. "And now it's empty," Rain said.

"Don't let him hear you say that, honey. He's still here. He's still with us."

Rain didn't know if she believed that but didn't dare disagree now. They remained silent in each other's arms. The light was fading in the little room.

Finally, Rain whispered, "I'm going to miss him so much."

"Me too, baby. Me too."

They held each other for a good hour more.

Outside, shadows lengthened. The sun felt heavy and tired from its long journey and began to sink below what passed for Old Town's skyline. Automatically, the streetlamp in front of the Inn clicked on.

Mother and daughter had managed to pull each other together. Rain, by this time, had a real stiff-upper-lip thing going. Iris was just starting to move past the shock and loss of her father's death to face a sudden wave of overwhelming details that had begun to cascade down upon her. *There's so much to arrange. A funeral. The headstone. A wake. And we still have guests to take care of.* Momentarily panicked, she stood and crossed to the door. Then she caught herself and turned back toward the one thing in her life that mattered more than any of it. "Will you be all right?" she asked.

"Someday," Rain said. "How about you?"

"I'm working on all right."

Rain understood and nodded. They both managed weak smiles. Then Iris left the room, closing the door behind her.

Rain was alone. Deeply, fundamentally alone. The room was dark now, but Rain didn't have the energy to turn on a light. She didn't have the energy to move. She continued to stare at the doorway as if her mother still stood there.

And then something was there. Something that bled through the door like gray smoke. Something that co-alesced into a figure. The Dark Man. The Dark Man from her dream. Black hair. Broad shoulders. Growing more distinct. She could see him now. Young, tall, with piercing black eyes that stared at her, riveted her to the bed. She tried to get her mind around what she was seeing. On this vision. He was wearing some kind of bomber jacket and maybe a military uniform; his black, black hair swooped up and back like hawk feathers. But she couldn't take it all in. Couldn't take *him* all in. He was translucent and glowed softly. And worse yet, she knew. She knew. *This isn't a dream! This isn't a dream!*

The Dark Man took a step forward, his hands reaching out for her.

And the spell was broken. She scurried back against her headboard and SCREAMED!!!

So little time had passed, Iris had barely taken three steps toward the stairs. Immediately, she swung back around and threw open her daughter's bedroom door.

Rain was still screaming. Iris rushed forward, in a near panic herself. "Rain, what is it?!!"

Rain watched her mother swing open the door. Watched her move toward the bed and in the process pass right through the Dark Man as if he wasn't there. Rain did the only thing she could. She screamed again.

The Dark Man reacted too. When Rain screamed the first time, he stopped dead in his tracks. When Iris passed through him, he actually looked stunned. He stared down at his own semitransparent body with a look of horror.

Iris wrapped her arms around Rain. Alonso suddenly appeared in the doorway behind the Dark Man. "Rain . . . ? Iris, what's wrong?!"

Rain pointed frantically at the Dark Man. "What do you mean what's wrong?!" She sounded hysterical.

Alonso looked behind him. *What's she pointing at?*

Iris watched helplessly as Rain pointed at Alonso and screamed, "There! Don't you see him?!"

Iris held her daughter tightly and tried to calm her, but her own confusion and fear was evident in her voice: "See who? Your father?"

"NO!"

Alonso took a step into the room. He was now standing an inch behind the Dark Man. "Rain, baby, try to calm down." His voice had the tone of one trying to talk a lunatic down off a ledge.

Now Callahan stood in the doorway. "What's going on?" he asked.

Without hesitating, Alonso turned and politely but firmly said, "Family business." Then he closed the door in Callahan's face.

Out in the hallway, Callahan bridled at the offense. For half a second, he considered busting the damn door down. But then he visibly shook off the impulse. *Ain't my business. Ain't my problem.* He shook his head. Shrugged. And moved off down the stairs.

Alonso had crossed to the bed. Rain's eyes never left the Dark Man. "You have to see him!" she yelled. "He's right there!"

And Iris: "Rain, please . . ."

Suddenly, the Dark Man leapt backward—or rather he seemed to be yanked backward—right through the closed door. His glow faded from the room, leaving it darker than ever.

Rain was breathing hard. Her parents whispered to her soothingly. But she did not feel soothed. She felt incensed. The moment the Dark Man vanished, her fear absolutely melted into anger. Without warning, she bolted away from her concerned parents and rushed the door. Pulled it open with so much force, it slammed into her bedroom wall. No dread. No hesitation. She was out in the corridor, ready to confront him. It. Whatever.

But there was nothing in the well-lit hallway. No one. No Dark Man. Nobody. Now, even the anger deserted her. "He's gone . . ."

Alonso was right behind her. He caught her up in his arms, a rag doll. She sounded confused, broken. "He was there . . . I saw him . . ."

Rain's father half-carried her back into her room. The only thing he could think to say was, "It's been a very hard day."

Iris helped him get their daughter into bed. "You just need some rest, baby. It'll all be better in the morning."

In the lobby, Callahan passed Ms. Vendaval without giving her so much as a glance. She turned her head to watch him go. When the door closed behind him, she smiled. Outside, he walked down the front steps of the Inn and paused to look up in the general direction of Rain's second-floor window. Then he stalked away. He had things to do.

CHAPTER SIX

FISHING

I thought we had things to do as well. But Maq had taken us off the big island to work the tourists on La Géante. When that had failed, he tried fishing from the Grande Jetée with a hook off his straw hat tied to a long piece of string dug out of his shirt pocket. This also offered little hope of success, since (although I'm not sure he noticed) he wasn't using any bait. I stared at him impatiently. I felt sure we should get back to San Próspero. But he ignored me, and given my recent track record, I wasn't about to run off to the Nitaino on my own.

Charlie, however, made two appearances there. When he had returned home, his mother had broken the news about 'Bastian. Immediately, he took off running. He knew what the old man meant to Rain. He pushed himself so hard that his calves started to burn and his lungs ached. His father's loose wristwatch bounced heavily on his arm. It wasn't the same thing, but he thought he knew how she was feeling. He thought maybe he could help.

He arrived at the Inn scant minutes after Callahan had left. In fact, he passed the big Australian on the street heading the other way. Neither paid any attention to the other. Charlie burst into the lobby, taking no more notice of Ms. Vendaval than Callahan had. She watched him bound up the front stairs. She smiled again and turned her attention back to the postcard rack. Though she wasn't likely to make a purchase, there was a picture of the ocean she particularly admired.

Charlie nearly made it to Rain, but Alonso stopped him. He had just left her room, and Charlie practically crashed into him at the head of the stairs. "Whoa. Slow down. Hold it."

"I came as soon—I wanted to—"

"I know, Charlie. You're a good friend. But this isn't the time. She's very upset. Her mother is with her now. She needs quiet."

"If I could just . . ."

"Tomorrow, Charlie. You'll see her tomorrow. She'll need you just as much then."

Alonso held Charlie's eyes until the boy looked away and nodded. "Okay," Charlie said. "Can you tell her I was here? Tell her . . ." There were so many thoughts in his head he couldn't possibly narrow them down into a coherent message.

But Alonso got the idea. "Of course," he said and placed a reassuring hand on Charlie's shoulder.

Charlie turned around, stuffed his hands in his pockets and descended the stairs. Alonso watched him go with no small amount of admiration. He usually took Charlie for granted. The kid had been underfoot for thirteen years. But now this kid was becoming a young man. And Alonso was gratified Rain had a friend she could count on. On the Ghosts, loyalty meant everything.

Charlie passed through the empty lobby and walked slowly home. He remembered his promise to call Miranda on her cell phone to let her know what had happened. He kept it brief, and she didn't keep him on the line. He ate dinner with his family in silence. Then he went to bed.

His second appearance came later.

Iris sat by Rain's side, stroking her forehead the way she had done when Rain was a little girl. She thought she might have to stay there all night, but her exhausted daughter drifted off after twenty minutes. Iris quietly left the room, locking the door behind her. Then, despite her own exhaustion and grief, she helped her husband organize her father's funeral for the next day.

Rain slept soundly until the dreams started again. There was no chase this time, no fear. She was simply standing in the lobby of the Nitaino Inn with Charlie there beside her. " 'Bastian's gone," she told him.

"I know," he said.

"I'm going to suffocate here. I can't breathe now."

"There's nothing left to keep either of us here," he said.

"Just the threat of death. If we don't finish high school, our parents'll kill us."

"Fine. We'll finish high school. But after that, we leave together." They were on Miranda's father's boat, sleek and quiet, leaving Próspero Bay behind. "Promise me you'll come with me when I go."

"I didn't even know you wanted to go."

"Promise me," he said.

Rain wondered where they would go, where they were going. . . . And who was piloting the boat? She turned. It was Ariel. No, it was Miranda. No, it was Marina Cortez. No. It was Ms. Vendaval. The Tall Woman smiled at Rain and said, "We're going to New York. There's so much to see. So much I want to show you there."

Rain said, "I don't even know you."

"I'm Ms. Vendaval from New York City. What else do you need to know?"

"Why would you help me?"

"I was a girl like you, don't you think? A little girl from a small town. I felt trapped, so I made a decision to leave. The when didn't matter. It might have taken me years. The important part was making the decision and sticking by it. I left when I could, as soon as I could. I left my small town for New York City. Now I'm not a little girl anymore. I'm tall and sophisticated. I wear nice clothes, and I've seen the world. There's nothing left for you here. What else do you need to know?"

Charlie said, "Promise me we'll leave."

Rain said, "He's gone. I have to, I don't know . . . pay my respects first."

Ms. Vendaval shrugged. Or maybe it was Marina or Miranda or Ariel. Or maybe it was her mother. "Pay your respects," she said. "Say good-bye to everyone on the island, if you must. Then leave it quite behind you. There's nothing left for you here."

Charlie said, "Promise me."

"He's gone," Rain said.

"Promise me."

"I promise," she said.

And on the Grande Jetée, without benefit of bait, Maq caught his own big fish. He used the last of his matches to light a fire on the beach just before the dawn. He roasted the fish on a flat rock and split half of it with me. I had had my doubts, but he was right again. It was really quite good.

CHAPTER SEVEN

A WAKE

It wasn't on the nightstand. She checked it again. Checked behind. On the floor. Under the bed. She went through the drawers.

Outside, it was a sunny Saturday morning. A cheerful, pleasant morning. Mild for September, it could easily be classified as a "lovely morning."

Inside, Rain, wearing a simple black sleeveless dress, tore through her room. She checked her dresser. Pulled clothes out of every drawer. Checked her desk. Under the desk. In the desk drawers. Back to the nightstand. "Where is it?" she said aloud.

"Where's what?" Alonso stood in the doorway, wearing his worn dark suit. The one he usually referred to as "my funeral suit." Usually. He watched his daughter pulling books off her shelf. "Where's what?" he repeated.

"Papa's armband. I left it on my nightstand, and I want to wear it for the . . ." She couldn't complete the sentence. Couldn't say the word. She threw her arms up in exasperation. "It's vanished."

"You'll have to look for it after. We can't be late."

Rain had her back to her father. Her head sank melodramatically. She grumbled something he couldn't hear. Something that on any other day he might have punished her for saying. Head still lowered, she turned and tramped past him. He stuck his tongue into his cheek. Took a deep breath and pulled the door closed. Automatically, he checked to make sure it was locked. (You learn to do that when you live at an Inn.) Then he followed his daughter down the stairs.

The Cacique family stood in the quiet tree-lined beauty of San Próspero Cemetery among people they loved. Charlie was there, straitjacketed into a coat and tie, offering a sympathetic smile. His mother, Adriana Dauphin, had given Rain a gentle kiss on the forehead. Charlie's older brother, Hank, and younger brother, Phil, who usually treated Rain with differing versions of contempt, just nodded to her nervously. Old Joe Charone, 'Bastian's oldest friend, gave Alonso an encouragingly firm handshake, before kissing Iris and Rain. He wore a coat and tie and the same special-occasion over-strong aftershave that 'Bastian would never wear again. Even Miller, who sometimes worked the boat with Rain's father, was there, foregoing a perfect day for surfing to pay his respects. His blond ponytail lay against the back of his corduroy sports coat.

Then there were three generations of Ibaras. Two of Jacksons. Four of Hernandezes. Et cetera. 'Bastian had lived a long life and made many friends. Iris leaned her entire body against her husband's and said, "He'd have liked this." Rain heard and frowned.

Maq and I kept our distance. We didn't exactly have a respectful change of clothes, but Maq removed his big straw hat and held it over his heart. Rain glanced back. He caught her eye and winked at her. She forced a smile and looked away.

A few lazy bees buzzed about, looking to pollinate. Father Lopez began to speak. Keeping my ears open, I wandered off among the familiar gravestones and vine-covered mausoleums. Some were neatly kept. Others had been overgrown for centuries. Most were empty of anything that mattered to me, but they were pleasant reminders of smiling faces, kind voices and rich smells. Off to the side was a small pet cemetery where I could easily have spent the entire day.

The good Father kept his sermon short. But it

seemed to me he could have skipped it altogether. A pleasant breeze and the swaying, skipping shadows of leaves on the trees bespoke a better epitaph for old 'Bastian Bohique than any man's words ever could.

Still, before Rain knew it, she was back at the Inn. Friends and loved ones milled around the lobby and dining room, eating food, offering condolences, telling 'Bastian stories. There were too many people for the space. Too many people touching her face or shoulder. Kissing her cheek or her forehead. Stopping their tales when she came near. Rain felt like she was overheating. She couldn't eat. Could barely generate mumbled responses to each repetitive show of concern. She began to slowly navigate through the crowd toward the front stairs. She wanted to evaporate to the upper stories and listen to her iPod or her father's rock CDs or 'Bastian's old jazz LPs on the phonograph in his room. But reaching the bottom step, she immediately knew she couldn't go into his room. So she stood there, vaguely paralyzed.

The front door opened. It was Mr. Chung and Ms. Ellis-Chung. Tourists, guests of the Inn, backlit by the sun, standing there, wondering what kind of party they had been missing. They held the door open as they considered the somber, whispering crowd. And Rain bolted. Out the door. Outside. Away.

To the N.T.Z. of course. Where else could she go? Her good shoes hidden away where she and Charlie had stowed the bicycles two short nights and one horrific eternity ago, she slipped through the jungle in her knee-length black dress. She entered the clearing silently. And sat down on the sandstone slab overlooking the sea. She hugged her knees to her chest and finally began to breathe again.

Time passed. And Charlie was there. She didn't need to look back. She just slowly became aware of his presence behind her. Without turning, she nodded once. And he sat down on the slab next to her, still wearing his Sunday clothes, even his shoes. They sat there quietly, watching the ocean. Watching the sun move down the sky. They never spoke or even looked at each other. But she was glad he came. And he was glad to be with her.

Hours later found them in the exact same spot, practically holding the same pose. Rain had lowered her bare feet over the cliffside, and was gently letting them swing with the breeze. The sun sank into the ocean. The sunset was stunning. The end of a beautiful day on the Ghosts.

And still they maintained their vigil. Eventually, Rain felt moonlight wash over her body. Cooling and soothing her brittle fever from the wake. She stirred.

Charlie turned his head toward her. "I just had to get away," she said. As if he had just caught up with her and hadn't spent half a day beside her.

"It's okay."

She stood up. He did too. She smiled sadly, leaned in and gave him a peck on the cheek. "Thanks," she said.

Once again, he felt the rush of being near her. Full of self-loathing, he admonished, reproved, reprimanded and chided himself reproachfully. He just wanted to be her friend. *Now, of all times, just her friend.* But to his frustration, the buzz remained.

She turned toward the clearing, and her smile vanished; the color drained from her face. She and Charlie were surrounded. Where had they come from? Who were they? What were they? A barely audible *no* escaped her lips, and she started to back away . . . nearly stepping right off the cliff.

"Rain! Careful!!" A panicked Charlie grabbed hold of her, steadied her. He glanced back over his shoulder and down. It was a long way to the bottom. He looked at her profile. She hadn't even registered the cliff. *What the hell is she looking at?*

Spirits. Ghosts. Translucent. Glowing. Standing in a semicircle around the N.T.Z. Rain was hyperventilating, desperate not to lose it completely. *All these tourists do NOT belong here,* she thought. She counted them.

There were eight of them. She counted again. Still eight. The counting helped calm her. Helped focus her. There had seemed to be so many at first. But no, it was a finite number of dead folk. Fixed and unchanging. At least for now. She scanned their shimmering faces. It was hard to clearly discern their features, but she was soon convinced. The Dark Man wasn't there. These were new ghosts. All men. All dressed in bomber jackets and some kind of uniform. They looked to her like old-fashioned World War I flying aces or something.

Then, just as her breathing returned to normal, they started to approach. To close in around her and Charlie, who still had both hands locked tightly around her arm. She looked at him. He was clearly frightened, glancing back and forth between her and the clearing. *He sees them*, she thought. *Thank God, he sees them.*

Rain cringed involuntarily as the Eight drew closer. They began to point out to sea. Their lips were moving but no sound came forth. Rain studied their body language. They seemed to be begging, imploring. "What do they want?!"

Charlie was clearly freaked: "What? Who? Rain, what's wrong with you?"

She turned on him like a woman betrayed. "The ghosts! Don't tell me you can't see them?! You have to see them!"

He looked at her, followed her gaze and stared at the empty N.T.Z. Moonlight and a cold fire pit. That was all. He turned back to her and shook his head.

She stared at him. Then slowly her own head rotated toward the Eight, still pointing, reaching, begging for something beyond the cliff. Equal parts dread, fear and anger were at war within her. But anger was something she could hold on to. So anger won. She took a step forward. Charlie released her arm. The ghosts ignored her. She took another step. "Why me?" she said. "What do you want from me?!"

Reaching out to sea, the ghosts ignored her still, looking through her as if *she* were the transparent one, as if she were the ghost. Desperate, she took three fast steps toward the nearest spirit and reached out to him, shouting, "What do you want?!" Her hand passed right through him. There was no substance, just sensation. She had vaguely expected him to feel cold. But whatever stuff he was made of was warm and liquid, like the Caribbean. He was tall, but she tried to meet his gaze. His face was fluid, indistinct. But young. Maybe nineteen or twenty. *How could he be so young?* She stood right in front of him, waving her arm back and forth through his head.

He took no notice. But somewhere, not in her ears, but in the back of her mind, she heard him speak . . . or maybe just think. The whispered words, like the ghost, were liquid, were smoke. But a few of them registered: *Home . . . Send us home . . . Finish it . . . The mission . . . Help us . . .*

It was her turn to beg, to implore. "Stop it! I can't help you!"

Finally, the spirit acknowledged her presence. He lowered his head. His eyes locked onto hers. Solid black and hard as jewels. She wanted to run away, but those eyes froze her in place. He reached out. Put a hand of smoke and liquid into her chest and spoke again, spoke to her. *Send us home!* His voice was the night wind blowing sand across the beach. Quiet, dry, steady, insistent and impossible to hold on to. And again, *Send us home!*

It was all too much. She shut her eyes. Screwed them shut against the young ghost, against all of the Eight. Charlie watched her body coil into a kind of standing fetal position. Finally, she screamed: "GO AWAY!!"

Silence. The whispering stopped. Slowly and with great trepidation, she raised her head. The young ghost was gone. The Eight were gone. She turned a full circle. The clearing was empty. Moonlight. A cold fire pit. A cliff. Rain Cacique. And Charlie Dauphin, staring at his lunatic best friend.

She felt like a lunatic. Or one step from lunacy at

most. She looked at Charlie. He hadn't seen anything. "Rain?" he said.

She shook her head, muttering to herself, "Maybe I am losing it. You can't see them. No one can."

Charlie wanted to say something helpful, so: "It's grief. Playing tricks on you. It has to be."

She nodded absently. *That's right. That's all it is.* He took her hand and squeezed it. She managed a smile. Then strangely disappointed, she walked with him into the jungle.

CHAPTER EIGHT

GRAVE

Rain recovered her shoes from behind the ferns. Charlie watched intently as she slipped them on and emerged into the light of the Camino.

"Kinda dressy for the N.T.Z."

Rain and Charlie turned to see Marina Cortez watching them with amusement. "What are you guys, having candlelight dinners up there?" She was sitting next to Ramon Hernandez on the front bench seat of his convertible. He leaned over to whisper something in her ear. Rain didn't have to be a psychic to guess what he was saying. Ramon had been at the funeral and the wake with his parents, grandparents, sisters, in-laws, nieces and a nephew. As Marina's expression changed from mirth to sympathy, Rain once again felt the weight of everyone on the islands knowing her business.

Marina climbed up onto her knees and leaned out of the car, saying, "Rain, I'm sorry. I didn't know."

Rain didn't want pity or even compassion right now. Other people's emotions felt like a burden. Created expectations for how she was supposed to respond in turn. "It's okay," she said flatly, which was all she could manage.

"It's not okay. I know. Look, why don't you guys hang with us tonight." Then, after the fact, Marina glanced toward Ramon for confirmation. He didn't look thrilled. Clearly, he'd been hoping for some alone time with the pretty girl from Malas Almas. But he wasn't a complete idiot. There really wasn't any way he could object.

"Yeah, sure. Climb in," he said, hoping his tone sounded inviting enough to fool Marina, but threatening enough to discourage Charlie at least.

But Charlie wasn't searching for nuances. This was an unprecedented opportunity. Seniors didn't invite eighth-graders to hang. If they could just be spotted driving around with Ramon by someone, anyone, from school, it would alter their entire status come Monday morning. Plus, it might serve to get Rain's mind off of, well, whatever.

"Not tonight," Rain said.

Marina would not be thwarted so easily. "Come on, come with us." She opened the door and slid closer to Ramon to make room in the front seat.

Ramon liked the sliding closer part, and his attitude improved, "Yeah, Cacique. Get in."

Charlie nudged Rain toward the car. "It's what you need," he whispered. "Blow off some steam. With *seniors . . .*"

It wasn't what Rain needed, and she knew it. But she felt defused. They were being so nice, and she couldn't come up with any peer-acceptable objection. She slid into the front seat next to Marina. "Thanks," she said, not meaning it very much.

It was only then that Charlie realized he wouldn't be sitting next to Rain. He stood over the others stupidly, until Ramon finally said, "Well, what are you waiting for? Climb in."

Charlie lurched over the chassis and tumbled into the backseat. Ramon put the car in gear, surreptitiously slipped an arm behind Marina's back and drove off.

There was an awkward silence. Then Marina turned abruptly to Rain and said, "You know, my older sister died last year."

"I didn't know," Rain said quickly. "I'm sorry." It was almost exactly what Marina had said to her two minutes earlier, but they were the only words Rain could find. Marina's revelation confused and upset Rain. The truth was she didn't know Marina Cortez very well at all. There was the age difference, and, besides, Marina lived two islands over. Rain saw her around sometimes, but they had no history together. *Now, we're sharing this?*

Ramon said, "Man, baby, I didn't know that either. Your sister? That sucks. Way worse than a grandfather."

And from Charlie: "Yeah, sorry, Marina."

Marina ignored the boys, keeping her focus on Rain. She said, "I didn't tell you to make you feel guilty. And I sure didn't tell you to compete. I just wanted you to know I understand what it feels like. I've been there. If you want to talk or if you just want to shut up, it's cool. I get it."

Rain just felt muddled. She didn't know what she wanted. Didn't know where they were going. Ramon was just cruising around, heading vaguely for the water. Charlie was desperately scanning the streets, still searching for that someone, anyone, to start the rumors flying at school.

Marina kept talking. Her voice was kind and soothing. "After she died, I felt like . . . my family . . . like they were putting me in a cage, you know? I started taking on her chores. Cooking the exact meals she used to cook for Mom and Dad and my brothers. It got to the point where I didn't even want to be around anyone that knew her. Or anyplace we had been together. That's when I started coming here every chance I got."

"Oh, yeah," Rain muttered sarcastically. "San Próspero rules."

Marina smiled. "Try hanging on Malas Almas. Makes San Próspero look like Vegas."

Rain considered that, then nodded. "And at least you were getting away."

"Exactly. You get it."

"I get it."

And Ramon: "Oh, me, too. Come June, I am gone. Mainland, babies. Miami Beach."

Charlie couldn't resist: "'Cause you haven't spent enough time in a tropical paradise?" Ramon flashed him an angry look in his rearview mirror that said, *Listen, scrub, you are here by the grace of me, so shut it!* Charlie got the message, lost the smile and sat way back in his seat.

Rain asked Marina, "What about you? After you graduate, I mean."

"College, hopefully. I'm going to apply to every school in every big cold ugly city I can find. If I get in any of them and get financial aid, then, sure, I'm gone too."

Charlie got brave again: "My brother Lew's a sophomore at Northwestern."

Ramon stopped the car at a red, and turned to face the backseat. Charlie winced, waiting for the order to hit the pavement. But Ramon had been a fan. "Lew Dauphin. Dude, he could move. Football scholarship?"

"Soccer," Charlie said, relieved. "But he tore up his knee. He's red-shirting."

"Man, I didn't know. That sucks." Marina and Rain stared at Ramon, then looked at each other and smiled just a bit, sharing a common thought. The guy had only one level of tragedy. 'Bastian's death. Marina's sister. Lew's knee. Ramon incidentally thought it all sucked.

The light changed, and Ramon drove on. "Your brother Hank's pretty good too. He'll start at corner-back, this year." Ramon glanced into his rearview again. "What about you? You goin' out for J.V.?"

Charlie considered numerous responses, before Rain cut off his options with, "He's in eighth grade. And he doesn't play football." Charlie suppressed a groan.

"That sucks," Ramon said, glancing with disapproval into his mirror.

From where I was standing, the conversation had become frustrating. Ramon was still heading vaguely toward the water, but Rain was going nowhere. Maq probably wouldn't have approved of my plan, but he was snoring under his hat on a bus bench and unavailable for consultation. So I swallowed hard, lowered my head and ran out into the street.

Ramon had only just turned his attention back to the road and nearly didn't see me at all. Marina froze in her seat. But Rain, bless her, shouted, "Look out!" She reached across Marina, grabbed the wheel and wrenched it to the right. The convertible squealed as it veered away from me and down Old Plantation Road.

You could hear the steel-drum band of their hearts pounding inside the car. Ramon, both hands on the wheel now, recovered and muttered, "I wasn't going to hit him."

Marina said, "Let's just turn around and head for the—"

"Stop!" It was Rain. A jittery Ramon hit the brakes and skidded to a stop about a hundred yards beyond the main gate to San Próspero Cemetery. Rain had turned around in her seat. The steel drums had taken on their own beat, their own edge. The cemetery. If she was seeing ghosts, she'd be sure to see some here. And not just any ghosts. Not just strangers, but the one ghost she'd actually like to see, wish to see. 'Bastian.

Charlie said, "Rain?"

"I want to go in. I was in a fog this morning. I want to go in now." She opened the passenger door and got out. Charlie climbed onto the trunk and followed. Ramon looked at Marina and shrugged. Finally, they were alone. His arm began to slide back around her shoulder, but she slipped away to pursue Rain.

Rain pushed on the unlocked iron gate. It was always oiled before a funeral, so it glided open smoothly. Charlie caught up to her right elbow, effortlessly. (Like his brothers, he could move when he wanted to.) They crossed into the moonlit graveyard side by side. "Are you sure about this?" he asked.

"Yes."

He watched her eyes shoot back and forth in her head, looking for ghosts. Before he knew it, he was doing the same. Marina materialized on Rain's left. *She looks spooked too,* Charlie thought.

"Hey, wait up!" Ramon shouted, too loud for this hallowed ground. He nearly tripped over a tombstone, trying to catch up. Marina shushed him.

I crept up to the gate and watched from the shadows. Soon all five of us were jerking our heads back and forth at every breath of the wind, every rustle of a leaf. All on the lookout for ghosts that some of us wouldn't recognize if they walked right through us.

Rain was the only one actually hoping for an apparition. The steel drums were warm and tangy and familiar in her head. They brought comfort. Gave her the confidence to face anything. And really, wouldn't it be better to have evidence that she wasn't insane? Wouldn't it be better to see a ghost, as long as it was the right ghost?

She stopped in front of the two graves with their single large stone, purchased nearly two decades ago when her grandmother had died. ROSE & SEBASTIAN BOHIQUE. LOVING PARTNERS. LOVING PARENTS. And the dates. Three old dates, from long before Rain was born. And one new date. Yesterday. *Only yesterday.* She knelt before the soft clean earth that covered 'Bastian's coffin. Only this morning—*only this morning*—she had moved like an automaton to drop a single rose on that coffin before this soft clean earth covered flower, box and man.

She closed her eyes. Flanked on four sides by Charlie, Marina, Ramon and the tombstone (all of whom seemed on full alert against the very spectres Rain was praying for), Rain willed her grandfather to appear. The drums built to a climax. She felt certain. When she opened her eyes, he would be there . . . and the world would make sense again.

But he wasn't there. Her almond eyes opened to find only Charlie, Marina, Ramon and the tombstone. Crestfallen, she looked to the well-kept grass that covered her grandmother's resting place. But she had never known

Rose Bohique and didn't really expect her to show. If 'Bastian wouldn't come, then why would Rose? And if 'Bastian wouldn't appear, than why would any spirit appear to her? *They wouldn't,* she decided. The drums were silent, and she felt like an idiot, like a child, standing in a cemetery at night. Like Linus van Pelt waiting for the Great Pumpkin to rise from the most sincere pumpkin patch.

She got to her feet. Charlie steadied her, but she shook him off. "Let's get out of here," she said.

"Gladly"—from Ramon, and he led the way back to the gate.

This time, Rain got into the backseat with Charlie. Marina was trying to be supportive. "It helps to see something concrete sometimes. To make it real, you know?"

Charlie nodded. Rain just sulked. "Can you take me home now," she said. Marina looked at Ramon, who nodded and turned the car around. They drove past me without noticing. Turned off Old Plantation Road and drove past Maq on his bench, without seeing or waking him. If nothing else happened, they'd be back at the Inn in less than five minutes.

Five minutes for Rain to stew in her own juices. *There's no such thing as ghosts. You're a dope. Or a nutcase.* Marina would periodically turn around to look at the younger girl. Ramon was quiet, but even he was checking his rearview to see if Rain was okay. Charlie, who wanted to hold her, tried desperately to not even brush against her. Rain noticed none of it.

Trouble is, I saw them. I know I did. The Dark Man. The Eight. I saw them.

She remembered Charlie's words: *It's grief. Playing tricks on you. It has to be.*

In the backseat, she nodded absently to herself. *That's right. I'm grieving. I—*

But a new thought occurred, or rather an old one resurfaced. She stopped nodding and raised her eyes to meet Charlie's. She spoke aloud: "You said I was messed up because of 'Bastian. Grief was playing tricks on me, right?"

Marina practically turned around in her seat. Charlie answered carefully, "Yeah. That's right."

"Except I saw the first ghost *before* I started grieving!"

Marina said, "Excuse me?"

Charlie held her gaze. He recognized this expression. He'd just told her to turn right, and she was determined to go left.

"What if I'm not crazy?" she said. "What if it's all real? This started before I knew he was gone." He could see her searching her memory, see the lightbulb click on. "The night he gave me the *armband!* When I first put it on, I felt . . ." She struggled to remember, but the sensation slipped away, like water, like smoke. So she shook off the memory to focus on something concrete. "I have to find it. But where . . ."

She grabbed his arms, as if maybe he could tell her. But he didn't know what she was talking about. All he knew was that she was on fire. The cold moonlight shone in her eyes, but the light that reflected back burned. He didn't know "where" this was taking her. He just knew he'd follow.

She stared past him, like the Eight had stared past her. "Where, where, where?" Then her entire body went rigid. She smiled and growled.

"Callahan!"

CHAPTER NINE

SEARCHER

Rain had a master key that accessed every room in the Inn. It did not usually represent an awesome responsibility. Usually, it was a simple means to a mundane end. *Yippee, I get to change more sheets!* But tonight it felt different. Tonight, after knocking softly and calling out to confirm an empty room, it felt like she was using this key to cross an important threshold in her life. *"To unlock a door, you need two things: a key and someone who knows how to turn it."* The girl who turned this key and entered this room would never be the same again.

And typical of Rain, she didn't hesitate.

She immediately set to work. Each spring, the whole family did a thorough cleaning of every room. Rain had found some pretty goofy stuff secreted away and forgotten by long-gone guests—so she knew every possible hiding place. It helped that *this* guest had brought so little to the Inn. First off, she emptied the entire contents of his duffel onto the bed. Sorted through it. Went through every pocket. Nothing.

She checked inside the pillowcases. Then she looked under the bed. Next, she lifted the mattress, slid it halfway off the box spring. Most of the man's stuff fell onto the floor. She'd clean it up after. Cleaning and straightening was something at which she'd had a lot of practice. There was a little tear in the fabric covering the box spring. Not big enough for the armband to fit through, but just in case, she ripped it open wider and reached around inside. Nothing.

The drawers to the dresser and nightstand—she pulled all of them all the way out. Most were empty. None held anything of interest. She ran into the bathroom and scanned the counter. There was a can of shaving cream. She popped off the top and even tried twisting off the bottom, in case it was one of those fake cans that people put valuables in. Just to be safe, she squirted a ton of white foam into the sink. It was, as advertised, a can of shaving cream. She checked under the sink, in the tub, in the trash can, even inside the toilet bowl and tank. Nothing.

She reentered the bedroom. Pulled the furniture away from the walls, one piece at a time. She checked the little indentation where the phone plugged in behind the headboard. She turned over the chairs and the little table to see if her prize had been taped underneath. She ran her hands through the closed curtains. She picked up a chair and climbed up onto it to check the curtain rods. She scanned the ceiling. Nothing.

She stood in the center of the room, more confident than ever that he had taken the armband. And then she heard the footsteps.

The *clomping* of heavy boots on the stairs. She remembered that sound all too well from the night he had arrived. The night 'Bastian had died. She glanced around the wreck of the room. No way she gets it back together in the next six seconds. Or less. The footsteps stopped right outside the door.

Out in the corridor, Callahan didn't have the courtesy to fumble for his key. He took it out in one smooth motion and slipped it into the lock. His huge hand turned the knob.

Rain had time to think, *I am so dead* . . . before the door began to slide open.

It only took a glimpse for Callahan to know the room had been compromised. He swung the door open the rest of the way, ready to do battle with . . . No one. The room was a shambles. But no one was there. He cursed himself for being complacent. *Backwater island. Backwater Inn. But no excuse.* His eyes played toward the half-open bathroom door. As smoothly as he had slid out his key, he slid out a large jackknife from his boot. He snapped it open, shiny and sharp. Slowly and silently, he walked past the curtained French doors and approached the bathroom.

Fortunately, Rain was out on the balcony, or rather, hanging off it from the wrought-iron balcony rail. She figured it was a pretty good hiding place. Even if he looked out the French doors, even if he stepped through them onto the balcony, barely her hands would be visible in the moonlight.

She glanced down. A one-story drop into the Inn's back garden. Could she jump? She wasn't sure there was another option, since she wasn't a hundred percent sure she could pull herself back up even if she wanted to— and it might not matter since *he* might not leave the room again 'til morning, and she knew she couldn't hang there all night.

But she could hang a bit longer. Maybe he'd rush out of the room to complain to her parents, and she could climb back up and slip out and across the hall to her own room while he was gone. Her parents would be very upset. They might even call the police. Maybe the police would find the armband. And then she thought, *Maybe it's out here!* She peered in the dim light around the balcony. He could have taped the thing anywhere— even beneath the balcony itself. She strained her eyes searching for some indication of its presence. . . .

Then two huge hands reached down and grabbed her small ones, yanking her bodily upward in one impressive motion. Before she knew what was happening her arms were sore and her feet had touched down on the terrace. Before she could react to that, Callahan had pulled her back through the French doors and into his room.

When he saw it was the girl and no threat, the knife had gone back into his boot. But he wouldn't let go of her and tightened his grip until her hands felt like they were being crushed. He half-leaned down, half-reeled her in, until his face was nose-to-nose with hers; she could feel his hot breath, see every furious line etched on his countenance. "Made a mistake, girlie! No one messes with Callahan!"

Still she would not back down: "Well, no one steals from me! Give me back my armband!" Callahan didn't react, which was telling, she thought. *No confusion; he knows I'm onto him!*

Alonso, who had come up the stairs to check on his wayward child, found the door to the guest room wide open. He could hear the shouting. He appeared in the doorway, already asking, "What is going—" But he didn't finish that sentence. He saw the big man, saw Rain and immediately rushed in. "Take your hands off my daughter!" Ready for a fight, he separated Rain and the stranger.

Callahan sized up his new opposition in less than a second. Alonso Cacique was shorter, but still easily six feet tall. His frame was slim but well-muscled. (Sixteen years on a boat'll do that.) Plus he was a bear fighting to protect his cub. Still Callahan knew he could take the innkeeper. And just for the temporary satisfaction of acting, of doing, of feeling his knuckles striking the other man's jawbone, Callahan was on the verge of throwing that first punch. But he managed to strangle the impulse. Instead, he took a step back to reduce the temptation and swept his hand out to indicate the condition of his room. "Look what she did here!" he shouted. "She was rifling through my gear!"

"He stole Papa's armband! I saw him leaving my room!"

Callahan scowled at her with contempt. "You find it?"

Rain looked away.

"'Course not," Callahan continued. He then turned out all his pockets and patted himself down for her benefit. "'Cause I don't have it."

Alonso glanced up at Callahan's smirking face and strangled his own impulse to do something manly. Then he looked around the demolished room. *The guy's a jerk. But . . .* He turned to his daughter and with just the appropriate amount of disappointment in his voice, said, "Rain, I think you'd better apologize."

Rain stood there. She didn't move or speak for a long time. She wasn't looking at anything. Just building up steam. Finally: "NO! He took it! I know he did!"

She bolted out of the room. From where the men stood, they heard her bedroom door open and quickly slam shut. A very tired Alonso turned to face Callahan. He sighed. "I'm sorry about that. It's her grandfather. She's taken it pretty hard. And it hasn't helped that she lost something he gave her."

"No excuse," Callahan growled.

"Perhaps under the circumstances, I should arrange accommodations for you elsewhere."

Callahan suddenly looked insecure. His tongue ran over his lower lip nervously and his eyes twitched back and forth. When he responded, it was with a new conciliatory tone. Deferential, even. "Don't get carried away. Checking out tomorrow night anyhow. Can make allowances. Grieving kid. Tough break." He heard himself rambling and swallowed to get a grip on his big mouth. "Think I'll stay put," he said with finality.

Rain heard it all. The backpedaling. The nervousness. The determination to stay. All of it. She pressed against the inside of her bedroom door. The same door she had immediately cracked open after intentionally slamming it shut for effect. (Being known as the family Drama Queen had its advantages.) She listened as her father offered to clean up the mess and heard Callahan decline.

And she knew. He was connected to all of it. The armband. 'Bastian's death. The Dark Man. The Eight. She had no idea how it all fit together. But she knew Callahan was in the middle of it.

And she was almost right.

CHAPTER TEN

IN BLACK AND WHITE

That night there were no ghosts, no Eight, no Dark Man. Just the conviction that Callahan was responsible for it all. Having someone to blame was a great relief. Rain slept soundly.

Then it was Sunday morning. One more day before school started. It was almost unimaginable that she should be expected to return to class after all that had happened. She looked out the window. Hazy. She took a shower and tried to summon up a song to play in her head. An instrument even. But nothing would stick. Everything was gray, inside and out. She took her time getting dressed, took even longer to dry, brush and braid her hair into its long, thick, black rope. She had a pretty good idea of what was waiting for her downstairs and was in no hurry to face it.

Eventually, though . . .

She entered the kitchen, wearing her standard uniform of shorts, T-shirt, deck shoes and no socks, and was surprised to see her father preparing breakfast. That wasn't how labor was divided at the Nitaino. He silently watched her hesitant approach. Then he put down his spatula and held out a hand. "The key."

"I won't use it again. There's no point. He's hidden the armband somewhere else."

Alonso frowned. That wasn't the answer he was looking for. His hand didn't move. "I'm not going to argue with you, Rain. Give me the key."

She took out her key chain and started to remove the master. Her voice slipped into a whine: "Great. How am I supposed to do my Sunday chores without it?"

Alonso shoved the key in his pocket and spoke quietly as he fished around in it. "No chores for you today. Make sure you have everything you need for school tomorrow. Paper, notebooks. Pencils. Here." He handed her a twenty-dollar bill. "I'm not expecting change."

She stared at him with mouth agape. *This is my punishment? No chores and free money?*

He saw her reaction. "It's been a difficult few days,

Rain. Make sure you have your supplies. Then you can have the afternoon."

"Okay. Thanks."

She turned to go, turned back. "Where's Mom?"

"Upstairs. In 'Bastian's room."

Rain flinched. "What's she doing up there?"

He shrugged.

Rain nodded absently and left the kitchen. A heartbeat later, she poked her head back in and stared at him.

"What?" he said.

"Don't ever die, okay?"

"Okay, baby."

"Promise."

"Sure."

"Good."

She left again. He listened to her light footsteps dancing up the back stairs. Then he picked up the spatula.

Rain peeked into her grandfather's bedroom. Her mother was sitting on the bed surrounded by a half-dozen open cardboard boxes. Piles of clothes and old photographs were scattered everywhere.

Rain hesitated at the threshold, another threshold. But this one she didn't want to cross. *He's not here anymore.*

Iris idly unfolded a shirt from one pile and refolded it atop another. After a bit, she felt her daughter's eyes.

She lifted her head and smiled wistfully. "I'm just sorting through his things. I don't know what to do with this room."

Rain winced. "Can't we leave it as is?"

"I'm not sure he'd like that. I just don't know."

Rain considered that. *What would he want? A museum? A pit stop for still more tourists?*

"Can I have his room?"

Iris looked up again. Momentarily, Rain wondered who had spoken, who would make such an audacious request. It took seconds before she realized she had done it. Did she really want to live up here? *Would he approve?*

Her mother seemed to be considering the same things. Finally, she took a deep breath and said, "We can discuss it." Which meant *not now*.

Rain looked around from the doorway, craning her neck into the far corners, looking for some sign that she was welcome. Nothing spoke to her, but eventually she began to feel silly standing out in the hall. She stumbled in. Her mother had resumed her redistributions and took no notice. Rain tried to affect nonchalance as she wandered about the room. *It's bigger than mine.* The thought left her feeling immediately guilty. She didn't want to want it that way. *It's not across the hall from Callahan.* Another thought unbidden. Her face tightened.

No. I'll stay across from him. He's not getting away with this. Whatever *this* was.

Rain paused to look down at 'Bastian's old Spanish desk. An antique map of the Ghost Keys was unrolled flat on the dark wood and held in place by two paperweights: a steel-cased compass and her grandfather's homemade astrolabe. He had tried to teach her to use both when she was nine. She had mastered the compass easily enough, but the astrolabe was beyond her then. Now she didn't remember what it was even for. *A good paperweight though.*

She studied the map. It suddenly struck her that the islands were correctly labeled: "The Ghost Keys" and not "The Prospero Keys." *A local made this map,* she thought. She found the legend and a date, "Summer, 1799." *A very old local.*

Rain crossed to the bed and peeked inside an open box. A faded embroidered pillow lay on top. "What's this?" she asked and pulled it out.

Her mother paused to look. She gently took the pillow from Rain. It had been white once with irises neatly stitched into the cotton fabric. Now the white had yellowed and there was a brown water stain across the back. "Your Grandma Rose made this. When I was little I wouldn't go to sleep without it." Iris shook her head in something like amazement. "I had no idea Dad kept this."

"He was very sentimental."

"I suppose. I never thought of him that way. To me, he was this dashing rake. Like a pirate in an old movie."

Rain tilted her head and gave her mother an incredulous look.

Iris tilted her head right back. "I know. That sounds silly to you. But you only knew him as a very old man. He was so handsome, Rain. He wasn't young when he had me, but even when I was your age all my friends still had big crushes on him. Ask Charlie's mom."

Now Rain looked ill. "Mrs. Dauphin had a crush on Papa?"

Rain's mother considered this for a moment and soon her expression mirrored Rain's. "Yeah, I thought it was creepy too."

Rain felt a desperate need to change the subject. She took another look inside the box, reached in and pulled out a glass-framed black and white photograph that had long ago begun to brown with age. She glanced at it. Men in front of an old airplane. She started to put it down on the bed, to reach deeper into the box. Then she froze.

Terrified, she slowly turned her head to look at the picture again. It was like seeing a ghost, and for Rain that wasn't just an expression. Men in front of an old airplane. Familiar men. The Eight. And standing in the center of the crowd: the Dark Man. To be sure, she silently counted the heads. One, two, three, four, five, six, seven, eight, nine, ten? She counted again. And a third time. It wasn't the Eight plus One Dark Man. It was the Eight plus One Dark Man plus one more. . . .

She studied each face carefully to see if she could find the extra body. The ghost who hadn't yet appeared. It wasn't hard. All the faces were young. Barely men at all. All looked familiar, but on closer inspection, she realized that the second man from the right in the lower row was sitting in a wheelchair. His forehead was bandaged. He wore a bomber jacket like the others, but it seemed to her that he was wearing his over pajamas and a robe. She studied the others. The Eight. The Dark Man. And now there was a tenth. *The Injured Party.* The phrase entered her head unbidden; she wasn't exactly sure what it meant or whether it applied. Maybe she had heard it on TV. But that was his name now. The Injured Party.

She peered up at her mother, who was staring at another framed picture. Rain held out her haunted photo. She saw her hands shaking and hoped her mom wouldn't notice. "What's this?" Rain asked—as flatly as she could.

Iris handed her picture to Rain and took possession of the other. Rain's eyes fell on the new image in her hand. It was familiar. A wedding photo with a gold embossed caption that read, SEBASTIAN & ROSE BOHIQUE. She looked at her grandfather and had to admit her mother was right. He *was* dashing. She tried to imagine him then. The pirate, the rake. She knew the story, more or less. 'Bastian had told his worshiping version many times. 'Bastian Bohique was a confirmed bachelor, stunned into submission by the lovely young Rose Nitaino. "She chased me, 'til I caught her," he would say. "She knew we were meant to be together." He had married late in life. In his fifties. The black and white picture clearly showed the gray hair at his temples. Rain kept a watchful eye on his face, as if he might wink back at her. Half her mind struggled to recognize the smiling old friend she knew. But half her mind was struggling with a different identification. Struggling so hard, she had all but forgotten the picture she had handed her mother.

And then, just as Iris spoke, Rain knew. "That's Dad here in the middle. Which box was this in? I've never seen it before."

The Dark Man. The Dark Man. The Dark Man was 'Bastian Bohique. The wedding picture spanned the gap between the young dark devil in the bomber jacket and the sweet old man with sparkling gray eyes. That ghost reaching for her in her bedroom hadn't been evil. Hadn't been a threat. He wasn't trying to hurt her. *It was Papa. He reached out to me, maybe needed me— and I screamed at him! Screamed until he left me alone forever.*

She felt like dissolving. And looked like she felt. Iris dropped the picture on the bed to steady her daughter. "Rain? My God, Rain, what's wrong?"

Rain stared wildly at her mother. At the picture in her own hand. At the smiling devil eyeing her from among the other ghosts on the bed. *That's why he wasn't there with the Eight at the N.T.Z. Why he wasn't with his friends. Or at the cemetery. I chased him off. Twice. He tried twice. I pulled away from him. I screamed. I yelled. I chased him out into the hall. He'll never come back now. I've lost him all over again!*

Tears came, followed quickly by great heaving sobs. Iris wrapped her arms around her shuddering child and began to rock her gently back and forth. Rain just kept repeating, "He won't ever come back. He won't ever come back again."

CHAPTER ELEVEN

THE FERRYMAN

It took a good half an hour for a tearful Iris to calm Rain down. The saving grace, as Rain saw it, was that her mother attributed this latest breakdown to general grief. She had no idea of the new guilt Rain was carrying. *'Bastian chose me. Not Mom, but me. And I sent him away forever.* Rain was sure her mother would never forgive her for that. So she could never find out. Rain struggled to control her breathing. To focus on something that didn't make her head spin.

Callahan.

In a strange way, he had become her mind's greatest ally. The anger she felt toward him was a tide washing everything else away. Fear, guilt, misery, they'd roll out to sea on the wave of his crime. She would get that armband back. 'Bastian's armband.

She forced herself to study the two photographs again. In the wedding picture, the armband peeked out from below his sleeve on his right wrist. But in the airplane shot, she couldn't see it. Maybe it was under the cuff of his bomber jacket. Or maybe he wasn't wearing it at all.

Iris watched her, and Rain soon became aware of the attention. Again, she held up the airplane photo and tried to keep her voice calm. "When was this taken?"

"I'm not sure. During World War Two, of course. You knew your granddad was a bomber pilot."

"I guess I did. Sort of. I knew he was in the war. Went to Europe. But I don't know how I knew. I can't remember him ever telling me or anything."

"No. Dad never talked about the war. Wouldn't talk about it."

"Do you recognize anyone else? Like this guy?" Rain pointed at the Injured Party. "Or anyone?"

Iris scanned each face over Rain's shoulder. Finally, she shook her head. "He never talked about any of it. Now it's lost."

Lost. Rain felt 'Bastian staring at her from the photograph. The Dark Man smiling and confident. Probably disgusted with her. She held the picture to her chest so she wouldn't have to look at that face. But she wouldn't let it go. Keeping it would be her penance . . . like the albatross in that *Mariner* poem they had studied last year. "Can I have this?" she asked, half hoping the answer would be no.

But Iris seemed pleased that Rain wanted it. She nodded to her daughter. Rain swallowed hard. *Careful what you wish for.* "I have to go get school stuff," she said. "Dad gave me money."

Iris gave her daughter a bookkeeper's stare. "We discussed that. Just make sure you get what you need before you spend the balance."

Rain smiled. She didn't need much. She had an old binder she could reuse by throwing out last year's notes. And she had all the math stuff—ruler, compass, protractor. All she'd need were a couple pencils, a couple pens, a highlighter, some paper and a new folder. That would last her through the first month or so. After that, if she needed something else she could always wheedle a bit more cash out of her parents. Education was important to them.

Rain kissed her mom and left. She was outside the Inn before she realized she was still clutching the photo. *'Bastian, the Eight, the Injured Party,* all pressing against her chest. Ghosts, memories, guilt. She didn't want to be alone with them. She beelined for Charlie's.

An hour later she had her supplies in a plastic bag and nearly fifteen dollars still in her pocket. She showed the picture to Charlie as they sat on a bench between palm trees, twenty yards from the edge of the beach, where two seagulls were fighting over the remains of a corn dog. A warm breeze slid along the shore, but Charlie had to suppress a shiver. His jaw hung open as Rain tried to explain: "See, the first ghost was 'Bastian . . ."

"Wait, wait, slow down."

"And these guys. These other eight guys were the ghosts I saw with you at the N.T.Z."

"Rain."

She pointed at the Injured Party. "I haven't seen him yet. Maybe that's tonight's special moment."

"You have not been seeing ghosts."

"Shut up. I have. It's not like I'm happy about it. Doesn't really matter if you believe me, anyway. . . ." She trailed off, thinking.

"What?" he asked, apprehensive.

"What if this last guy isn't dead? I mean maybe that's why he wasn't with the others. What if he's alive somewhere, living in Nebraska . . . or London." The prospect of the Injured Party living in Europe actually brought a smile to her face. "He could tell me something. I wish I knew his name."

Before his mind had time to censor the thought,

Charlie asked, "Have you looked on the back? My mom always writes names on the back."

Rain rolled her eyes as she absently flipped the framed picture over. "There's nothing there."

Charlie rolled his eyes right back at her. "Not the back of the frame. The back of the picture. Take it out."

Rain mentally kicked herself. She flipped aside the little tab and lifted the felt and cardboard backing away from the photograph. Sure enough, there were three lines of faded pencil scrawl. On top it read, *May 8, 1945.* Below that, names and initials. *Top: Billy Z., Pete G., Me, Harry C., Harry E.* And, *Bottom: Bear M., Ducky S., Lance P., Joey C., Tommy M.* She flipped the picture back and forth, attaching a name to every face. "Me" was her Papa 'Bastian. 'Bastian B. This was his scrawl. And the Injured Party? The man in the wheelchair? *Joey C.*

Rain frowned. "No last names. Guess he thought he'd remember. It's gonna be hard to search all of London for a Joey C. Not much help."

"Can I see him again?"

Rain turned the photo over once more. They both studied good old Joey. Old Joey. "Oh my God," she said, "you don't think?"

"I don't know," Charlie said, but she could tell from the slow way he shook his head that the same thought had crossed his mind. Down on the beach, one of the birds snatched up the last chunk of corn dog and took to the air; the other remained, pecking at the crumbs.

Rain stood up abruptly. "Let's go ask him. I mean they were best friends. Even if it's not him, he might know something. We should ask him."

"Ask him what? Whether he's being haunted too?"

"We'll just show him the picture. See what we get."

"Don't tell him anything that's going to get you committed, okay?"

"Whatever. Let's go."

She took off with the photo. Charlie stood and picked up *her* bag of school supplies. He chewed on the inside of his mouth.

"Come on!" she yelled.

And he followed.

They had to wait fifteen minutes for the Sycorax ferry to return. Rain got in line and spent ten of her father's dollars on their two tickets, which kept her occupied for a full three of those minutes. But during the last twelve, Charlie half thought she was going to jump in the water and swim for the boat. Finally, it arrived, but the boarding process was so slow and deliberate, Charlie was glad Rain wasn't armed.

They boarded. Rain ran upstairs to the pilot's cabin with Charlie on her heels. A big sign said NO ADMITTANCE. A smaller sign said, DO NOT DISTURB THE

PILOT. Rain ignored both and grabbed for the door handle. It was locked. She pounded on the glass.

Old Joe Charone, the ferryman, turned with a scowl. Then he saw his best friend's granddaughter and his face immediately softened. Rain shouted through the glass, "Can we talk to you?"

"I'm workin', Sweetie."

"I need to ask you something."

So inevitably, Joe opened yet another door for Rain Cacique. She and Charlie squeezed into the little cabin. Rain started to talk, but a horn sounded, cutting her off. Old Joe picked up his radio and said, "Pulling out."

Rain tried again, "Joe, I want to—"

"Let me get her clear of port, Sweetie, then we can talk."

Rain did not take a deep breath and wait. She held out the photograph, demanding "Have you seen it before?"

Old Joe glanced at the picture, barely. "Once or twice," he said, smiling. His focus immediately returned to the harbor, but he jerked his head to the left. Hanging from the bulkhead was another copy of the photo in an identical frame.

CHAPTER TWELVE

THE STORM

Charlie gulped. Rain looked about ready to pop. "Then it is you," she said. "You're the Injured— the guy in the wheelchair!"

"The *kid* in the wheelchair," Joe corrected. "Yeah, that's me. Tail Gunner Joey."

"And Papa?"

"Captain Sebastian Bohique. He was a real war hero, Sweetie. He was *my* hero."

"The others?"

"The crew of the *Island Belle*. Here, show me that again."

Rain held up the picture. Again, Joe merely glanced at it. But this time when he stared out to sea, his vision searched backward. He knew that photograph by heart.

He knew everything about those years by heart. "Across the top that's Lieutenant Billy Zekaris, our bombardier. And Pete Grier from Mississippi. He was top turret. Then your grandfather. And Big Harry Connors and Little Harry Eiling, our waist gunners. Kneeling down you got Lieutenant William 'Bear' Mitchell, our navigator. And Ducky Simpson, ball turret. Sergeant Lance Pedros, radio operator. Me. And Lieutenant Tommy McMinn, copilot."

Yet again, Rain studied the now familiar faces. 'Bastian's writing on the back—even seeing the Eight spirits in person—had done less to bring them back to life than Joe Charone's few nostalgia-laced words. She looked at young Joey C. Wounded but smiling—and now so obviously good Old Joe. And beside him, Tommy McMinn, the tall ghost who had "spoken" to her at the N.T.Z. Finally, her gaze returned to her grandfather. "And 'Bastian was the pilot?"

"Through twenty-five successful missions. Nine of them over Berlin. He kept us alive. We'd have followed him anywhere. In fact, we did."

"When was this taken? I mean I saw the date on the back, but—"

"V-E Day." Rain and Charlie exchanged looks and nervous shrugs. It was clear from Joe's tone that this was something he thought both kids should know. He looked at them sternly. "Victory in Europe Day. Eighth of May, 1945. Day after the Nazis surrendered. There was still fighting in the Pacific. But we had flown our twenty-five runs. We were done. The war was over for us. Just one more mission left."

"What mission?"

"Something 'Bastian set up. When it mattered, your grandpa was rock solid. Serious. No foolin' around. But when it didn't matter, when nothing was at stake, he liked to have a good time. He liked attention too. For him they went together." Rain and Charlie stared at him blankly, so Joe clarified: "See, a little glory helped oil the gears for his fun."

He grinned at them. Still nothing. His grin turned sour with annoyance. "With women! You kids are old enough to hear this, right?"

"Yeah."

"Sure." But Charlie noticed Rain was wearing her icky-face.

"'Bastian loved the ladies. He used to say—and I certainly thought—that he'd never get tired of playing the field. Then of course, he met Rose, and everything changed."

"You're getting ahead of yourself," Rain said, anxious to put him back on topic.

"True, true. Where was I, Sweetie?"

"The mission. The last mission."

"Right. 'Bastian had this idea, see? It was unusual for a crew like ours to stay together from start to finish. There were injuries, illnesses, the occasional court-martial. Guys went on leave or they had enough combat points to get sent home."

Joe's tongue took a quick circuit around his lips. "And there were fatalities, you know?" This time, he didn't look at the two kids to make sure they understood. He knew they couldn't. Not really. Not the way he did. Not at their age. Not in the world they lived in now. *But that's a good thing,* he reminded himself. *That's why we fought.*

He searched his mind for his train of thought. Caught it and boarded. "But here we were—ten of us—still together after twenty-five sorties. I got a little chopped up on that last flight, but we were all alive and eager to head back to the States. 'Bastian just wanted a little fanfare for the journey.

"So he talked to the brass and convinced them we could still be of use to the war effort. They sent the *Belle* on a tour of the States to help sell War Bonds. There were ten stops. One for every member of the crew. We'd each get a chance to be the big man in our own hometown, or at least at the closest airfield."

Rain looked down at the *Belle*'s crew in her hand. In

her mind, the flashbulb went off and the ten sepia-toned men came to life, shaking hands, patting each other on the back. Everyone's extra solicitous of the injured tail gunner, until the young man growls, "Leave me alone. I'm fine, see?" Then their captain steps forward, tilts his hat back with casual arrogance and says, "Boys, have I got a surprise for you. . . ."

"Lance and Tommy and Pete, they didn't like the idea. They just wanted to go home and stay home. But it sounded good to the rest of us heroes, and even the naysayers weren't gonna say nay to 'Bastian. Heck, I was so excited I talked the docs into letting me go along, head injury or no head injury. 'Course I had pneumonia by the time we got to New York—that's where I'm from, you know; my dad piloted the Staten Island Ferry for forty-three years."

"So you missed the rest of the mission," Rain said.

Old Joe lapsed into silence, allowing his eyes to gaze inward again. Trying to fill the void, Charlie volunteered, "Sorry."

Joe chuckled ruefully and removed his Sycorax pilot's cap. He rubbed a pudgy hand over his sweating weathered face and through his thin gray hair. He replaced the cap. Rain watched his tongue sweep his lips over and over. The small humid room smelled of oil, the sea and 'Bastian's aftershave. The smells pushed in on

Joe and Rain and Charlie, tightened around them, close. Joe spoke again, but he still wasn't ready to proceed. "We're docking at Sycorax, and I need to concentrate. Go get some air, and we can finish talkin' on the trip back."

Rain tried to make room for his memories: "Something happened after New York. Something you missed."

Joe nodded curtly. "I'll tell you on the way back." It was clearly the final word. Rain wasn't good with final words. Her mouth opened in protest.

Joe growled to cut her off, "On the way back!" He looked sick. Dizzy.

Reluctantly, Rain allowed Charlie to pull her out of the cabin. They retreated to the deck, where Charlie seized the moment and handed her back her school supplies. Rain slipped the framed photo of the *Island Belle*'s crew into the shopping bag. Neither spoke; they just leaned on the rail as Joe gently glided the hulking ferry into its Sycorax Island berth.

Suddenly, Charlie perked up. "Hey, Miranda!"

Rain looked around but didn't—

"Charlie?!" Rain followed the voice and spotted their new friend. She was walking along the wide pier with that Ariel following a few feet behind her. The two kept pace with the ferry as it slowly docked. "What are you guys doing here?" Miranda shouted.

Chasing ghosts, thought Rain.

Charlie answered quickly: "Just taking a boat ride. How 'bout you? You working here?"

"I live here."

Rain and Charlie exchanged another odd look. Rain said quietly, "Nobody lives on Sycorax." It was largely true. Sycorax was the Ghosts' only privately held island, the 100 percent property of Sycorax Inc. Lots of people worked on Sycorax—at the processing plants or the factories. Old Joe ferried them over every morning and ferried them home to San Próspero every night. *But who would live here?* Rain wondered.

The ferryboat stopped with a lurch. Miranda called up to them: "Are you coming ashore?"

"We can't," Rain said. Even at this distance, she could sense Miranda's disappointment. "But we'll see you tonight at the party, right?"

Miranda smiled and nodded. She hesitated before speaking again and her smile saddened. "Rain, I'm so sorry about your grandfather. I didn't know if I should come to the funeral. I mean we haven't known each other very long. I didn't know if it was appropriate. . . ."

"It's okay," Rain said. "There were too many people anyway. I booked early."

Charlie piped in, "It's true. She ditched."

Movement behind her caught Rain's eye. She turned and saw new passengers boarding. She was immediately restless. She wanted—needed—to get back to Joe. She turned to Miranda. "We have to talk to the pilot. I'll see you later." And like a ghost, Rain vanished from the railing.

Not for the first time, Charlie felt the need to apologize for his single-minded friend. "Sorry. She's like that."

"I've noticed."

"You'll get used to her. It's mostly worth it. Mostly." Miranda laughed.

Charlie looked back over his shoulder. Rain was probably already knocking on Joe's door. "Look, I have to catch up. See you tonight!"

"Okay. 'Bye." Miranda watched as Charlie backpedaled, waved and turned from the railing. Then he was gone too. She stood there for a moment, replaying the entire exchange in her mind. She was pretty sure they liked her. She just wasn't yet a part of their world.

As an afterthought, she turned to Ariel. The blond woman stood there like a work of art, a figure bursting with life that had been captured and held forever in a moment of time made fixed and permanent. But Miranda didn't take particular notice of that particular tension. She was used to her companion. "Can you take me back and forth to San Próspero tonight?"

Ariel, maintaining her resemblance to a marble statue, said nothing.

"My father won't mind," Miranda said.

Almost imperceptibly, Ariel nodded.

"Thanks." A pleased Miranda turned and watched the ferry pull away.

Charlie rapped twice on the door to the pilot's cabin. Joe reached back and opened it. Charlie slipped inside. Joe was talking. Rain stood there rapt.

"The *Belle*'s second-to-last stop was Oxford, Mississippi, which Pete said was 'a mule ride' from his Pa's farm. Lots of folks came out to see the local hero, his compadres and the *Island Belle*. Everyone was treated like royalty, see? The mayor hosted a barbecue. A big party. Pete's parents and his little brother were there, beaming at their boy. Pete really didn't want to leave them again. And by this time, a bunch of the men wanted to go home. Each stop on the tour had made them miss their old lives more and more.

"But 'Bastian wanted us to see the Keys before we all went our separate ways. He was proud of these islands and wanted to show his boys a good time, Ghost-style. 'One last mission,' he said, 'one last flight and you can all go home.'"

"But you weren't there," Rain interrupted, confused.

"No. I was still in New York. I was hoping to meet them down here."

"Then how do you—"

GREG WEISMAN

" 'Bastian told me. When it was over. All over. He said, 'I'll tell you exactly once, Joe. But don't ever ask me again.' And so he told me. The whole thing. What I'm telling you now. But we never talked about it again. Not the war. Not this. None of it. I moved down here. And we were friends. But as far as he was concerned, life began in 1946."

Rain nodded. Solemn. Joe's tongue took another sojourn around his lips.

"The *Belle* left Mississippi and headed southwest. She was supposed to land at the naval base over on Tío Samuel. Your grandfather was piloting. Tommy was riding shotgun. Bear Mitchell had set their course down below, but there wasn't much for him to do now except compose dirty limericks. Lance was at his station with the radio on, but no one was talking. Pete would stick his head into the cockpit every once in a while. It was a habit he'd picked up from being top turret gunner. The rest had nothing to do but sleep a little, if they could. A B-17 bomber is built for combat, not comfort. It's loud, uninsulated, cramped. I don't miss that. Just the guys.

"It was raining. They were flying into a storm. A day later that storm would be reclassified as a hurricane and dubbed *Santa Julia*, but the *Belle*'s crew had no idea then it would get that bad."

There was no music in Rain's head. No sound except

Joe's voice. But she could see it. 'Bastian at the controls. Tommy in the next seat. Pete leaning in. Rain beating down. Lightning lighting up the cockpit like a hundred flashbulbs. But no thunder. Not yet.

"It was a bumpy ride. But still no indication from the Navy that they should turn back. They got close. Real close. But Julia . . . Well, the way 'Bastian put it, Julia made her presence known. Lightning hit the wing. An engine caught fire. The *Belle* started to augur in. 'Bastian and Tommy fought to keep her aloft, but the gale flipped her right over. They went down between San Próspero and Tío Sam's.

"Sweetie, your granddad was the only survivor."

Rain looked at her Papa, hanging on the bulkhead amid his smiling crew.

Joe took a deep breath and finished. "Sebastian Bohique was not a man to harbor regrets. He figured you took what life gave you, made your choices and lived with 'em. But this was different, see? He felt he kept those boys from going home. I didn't blame him; the Navy didn't blame him; the Army Air Corps didn't blame him; even the families didn't blame him. But he blamed himself. That's the one regret he took to his grave."

CHAPTER THIRTEEN

THE LAST SUMMER RAIN

Rain and Charlie walked slowly down the beach under the late afternoon's waning sun. She spoke quietly, almost to herself. "It all makes sense now. 'Bastian appearing. His buddies looking out to sea. He needed to set things right; he needed my help, and I let him down."

"Rain . . ."

"But why appear to me? Why not to my mom? Or to Old Joe, who would have understood? Or to anyone who would have handled it better?"

She stopped, turned and stepped in front of a worried Charlie. "The armband's the key. I know it is. And that means if I can get it back, I may still be able to get *him* back."

Charlie looked miserable. "Rain, let it go. Come to the party tonight and forget all this. It's . . . it's nuts!"

"I know how it sounds, but . . ." She stopped, looked around helplessly, then attempted to gather her thoughts. When she spoke again, her voice sounded fragile in a way Charlie had never heard before. "My world got smaller without him in it."

He wanted to reach out, at least put a hand on her shoulder. But he was afraid and then surprised and vaguely electrified when she put *her* hands on *his* shoulders. "That last night before, before he . . . he said the armband would make me feel part of something larger. I don't know if I believed him then. But I believe him now. And I need you to believe too. I said I didn't, but I lied. I can't do this without you."

Charlie stared at her for a long moment with his mouth hanging open. *Does she get what she's asking? How am I supposed to believe* any *of this?* And yet despite himself, his mouth began to curve into a smile. "How can I help?" he said finally.

Rain smiled back. She linked her arm in his and propelled them both down the beach. "I don't have a clue," she said.

"Your magic number is fifty-seven," Maq said, employing just enough volume to grab the kids' attention. We were about thirty yards farther down the beach, entertaining tourists for quarters.

"Bernie, that's your age!" Maude Cohen squealed.

"Then that'll be a quarter," Maq replied. He smiled at me, and I smiled back, as Bernie Cohen, wearing a new but equally loud Hawaiian shirt, hurried to pull a quarter out of the pocket of his Bermuda shorts.

Eagerly anticipating her turn, Maude pushed at her fumbling husband. "Give him the quarter, Bernie." And when he had, she turned on Maq: "Now, do me!"

Maq tipped back his old straw hat. He grinned broadly at Maude. "Your magic number is 171."

Bernie, impressed, said, "Maude, that's your—"

"Just give him the quarter, Bernie."

Rain and Charlie approached. Maq absently called out, "Hey, Rain." And I watched him pocket the second quarter as a fuming Maude pulled her husband toward the parking lot.

"Hey, Maq," Rain said.

I was lying on my stomach on the sand, and Rain crouched down beside me, while Maq and Charlie exchanged greetings. She rubbed my head then scratched between my ears, asking, "And how is Opie today?" in a cutesy baby-talk voice. Coming from anyone else, I'd have been annoyed.

"Your magic number is nine, Rain."

"What?" She looked up, confused.

Maq started to back away up the beach. Reluctantly, I pushed myself up onto my feet and padded after him. He moved pretty fast for an old guy. I had to run to catch up.

"Your magic number's nine," he called back. "And I'm giving you that for free."

Perplexed, she remained in mid-crouch for an easy ten seconds, watching us skip along the water's edge among the baby waves in the fading light. Finally she stood and faced Charlie. "Is it me or has my life gone totally strange all of a sudden?"

"Option C," he answered evenly. "All of the above."

They made their way back to the Inn. The sun was setting and a fine mist had swept in from the ocean. Someone somewhere was eating popcorn; its carnival smell drifted in with the slight breeze. Charlie paused on the Inn's front steps and held out his hand. Raindrops dotted his skin. He said morosely, "Rain's gonna spoil the party."

Rain looked at him. He said, "And, yes, I do mean you." She stuck out her tongue.

Smiling, they entered the lobby, and Rain's smile

froze. Callahan was checking out, settling his tab with Rain's mother. Rain's entire body stiffened. She glowered at him as hard as she could. He glanced her way, grunted dismissively and turned back to Iris. "Hi," Rain said to her mom, while trying to put just the right amount of challenge into the word for Callahan. "Hi" was a tough word to make challenging.

Nevertheless, Iris noticed the glowering and the tone and said pointedly, "Good news, honey. I found this in the laundry." And lo and behold, she held out the armband!

Rain's eyes went wide. A huge grin leapt onto her face. Joyously, she rushed forward, saying, "Mom, you're terrific!" But before she could reach the prize, Callahan snagged it out of Iris' hand.

He held the armband aloft, out of Rain's reach. "Someone owes someone an apology," he said.

Rain seethed. But she looked around the room. Charlie did one of his eyebrow shrug things. Iris clearly didn't like Callahan's style, but she wasn't defending Rain either. That meant Rain would have to apologize. So Rain took a deep breath and begrudgingly, painfully spoke. "I'm sorry I accused you."

Callahan smugly handed the armband to Rain. "Better," he said. He picked up his duffel and headed for the front door. Dripping with sarcasm, he said,

"Thanks for the hospitality." Then he stepped outside and let the door close behind him.

Rain shook her head. *He didn't take the armband.* She could barely believe it. *But I know he was up to something.* As she slid the cold metal of the armband onto her left biceps, she moved to the bay window overlooking the street. Outside it was dark and raining. Callahan paused to adjust his collar. The streetlight clicked on above him. He hefted his duffel onto his shoulder and started down the street.

Rain watched him pass from beneath the lamp. Yet there was another source of light. . . . The duffel itself was faintly glowing! Rain inhaled quickly as the Dark Man—'Bastian's ghost—materialized from inside the duffel bag!

Rain put her hands up to the window. She made eye contact with her semitransparent grandfather. He reached out to her. And then suddenly, he was yanked away. Rain's eyes ping-ponged between Callahan and 'Bastian. Callahan continued down Goodfellow Lane, seemingly unaware that he was somehow dragging 'Bastian behind him as if on an invisible chain.

Without looking, Rain reached back and grabbed a handful of Charlie's T-shirt. "C'mon," she whispered and pulled him toward the door.

It was still raining back at the docks. Callahan

walked down the gangplank to a large modified cabin cruiser with the words BOOTSTRAP and SYDNEY, AUS- TRALIA stenciled aft. Thirty yards away, Rain and Charlie watched, crouching behind a bus bench.

Rain stared as 'Bastian was drawn along behind Callahan. All Charlie saw was Callahan hefting his duffel onto the deck.

Callahan boarded. He unlocked a hatch, picked up the duffel and carried it below. The hatch shut behind him. Rain watched as 'Bastian's ghost was pulled beneath, melting down through the deck like rainwater.

"He *does* have it," Rain hissed.

"What?!"

She started to head for the boat. "I'll show you."

But Charlie grabbed her arm. "No! This has gone too far!"

Rain tried to remain calm, but it wasn't easy. The Eight had materialized around them forty seconds earlier. The ghosts stood in a circle, each consumed with pointing out to sea. Rain stepped back and put her hand against Pete Grier's. His plaintive voice sounded in her mind. *Complete the mission . . . Send us home! Please! Please!*

She said, "Charlie, they're here, and they need my help. And I can't help them if you don't help me."

Charlie watched Rain's eyes dart back and forth, saw her maintain her resolve (and maybe her sanity) through sheer force of will. He shook his head. "I said it's gone too far." He paused for effect. "Fortunately, too far is where I like to go."

She hugged him with enough force to expel air from his lungs. Before he had recovered (physically or emotionally), she yanked him through the ghosts and toward the boat.

Belowdecks on the *Bootstrap,* Callahan sat at a table, reviewing a chart of the Keys. The duffel sat on the floor at his feet. He circled a rendezvous point at sea then abruptly pushed back from the table and stood.

Simultaneously, Rain and Charlie were sneaking aboard the cruiser. They heard Callahan opening the hatch and quickly ducked down to hide behind the raised cabin. Callahan exited and let the hatch slam shut. He moved to the foredeck. The kids rounded the other way as Rain led Charlie toward the closed hatch. Charlie was borderline hyperventilating. Rain was barely breathing at all. She moved to the hatch and opened it with just the tiniest creak of a hinge. The sound seemed deafening, and they froze, waiting for Callahan's attack. Nothing happened. Rain's eyes met Charlie's. He mentally begged her to turn back. She instinctively knew this and responded—by descending belowdecks. Charlie quickly grabbed ahold of the hatch, followed his friend and gently closed it behind them.

Charlie stepped down into the main cabin. Rain stood there, surveying the scene, and Charlie scanned the room as well. One overhead light illuminated the small space, which was jam-packed with charts, shovels, scuba gear, even a harpoon gun. An open closet, stuffed with ropes, pitons and a metal detector, completed the picture. Charlie whispered, "What's this guy planning? The search for Atlantis?"

"The duffel? Where's the duffel?"

Above deck, Callahan was releasing the lines.

Below, Rain spotted his bag and rushed toward it. Charlie remained rooted to his spot. "What do you think's in there?" he asked, nervously looking over his shoulder at the closed hatch.

"'Bastian's armband." With one arm she was reaching into the bag, searching, searching.

Charlie turned back to her and stared at the gold armband on her other arm. "Uh, Rain, aren't you wearing—"

"Got it!"

Victorious, she pulled her right arm free of the duffel and held aloft a gold band identical to the one on her left. Her glory was short-lived. The boat's engine roared to life. Victory quickly turned to panic. "I think we better get out of here."

And Charlie: "Now there's an idea." As one, they rushed to look out a porthole. The dock was already sliding away. Within seconds, the *Bootstrap* had cleared its berth and was pulling out to sea. "A little late, maybe."

From the shore, Maq and I watched as the cruiser was shortly swallowed up by the rain and fog. Thunder rumbled in the distance. We shared a single thought: *Finally.*

CHAPTER FOURTEEN

'BASTIAN

The *Bootstrap* motored out beyond the harbor and the bay and proceeded northeast through the rain and choppy seas. At the helm, Callahan wore his customary contemptuous scowl, but he had no idea that two panicked teenagers were belowdecks, staring out a porthole at the fog-laden night. They turned toward each other. Rain whispered, "Now, what do we do?"

"Pray for an iceberg?" It was the best Charlie could come up with, plan-wise or gallows humor-wise. His eyes scanned around for some source of hope. Instead he found a source of confusion. Rain was wearing one armband, holding another. "Uh . . . are there supposed to be two of those?"

Rain looked down at the twin bands. It seemed to

take a second for them to register. Then some kind of internal switch got flipped, and she rushed back across the cabin to Callahan's duffel. She pulled the armband off her arm and stuffed it into the bag. Her mind was working out what must have happened as she relayed it in a low whisper to Charlie: "Callahan stole mine so he could replace it with a fake. That's why I couldn't find anything when I searched his room. And why he wouldn't leave the Nitaino. He had already taken the real armband out of the Inn so he could have a copy made, and he needed to stay put until it was finished." She pointed at the duffel. "He must have planted this phony in Mom's laundry today."

Charlie was wildly unconvinced. "Why?"

Rain shook her head. "I don't know."

She held up the real armband to examine it. It caught the light, which glimmered off the golden snakes, until they almost seemed to come to life in her hand. "Why would anyone go to all that trouble to steal a family heirloom . . . ?" She smiled slyly. ". . . And still fail." She slid it up her left arm, where the two serpents came to rest around her biceps like warm old friends.

Instantly, the armband no longer required the cabin's light. First came the lightning: a silent, double strike out at sea. Then to Rain (but not to Charlie) the armband began to glow softly white from within. And like a genie out of a bottle, the Dark Man materialized before his granddaughter's eyes. Gratefully, 'Bastian's spirit said, "Rain," his voice clear as a bell in her mind. "Raindrop."

"Papa," she whispered. They moved to embrace. But their arms passed right through each other. She reprimanded herself, *I knew that.* But she was disappointed nonetheless. She sadly pulled away.

His shoulders sank. "Sorry, I'm not all . . . here."

She reached forward to reassure him, barely remembering the lesson she had just learned in time to stop herself and pull away. *This is gonna take some getting used to.* "It's not important," she said aloud.

"At least you can hear me now," he said, too loud. Not at all like the smoky voices of Tommy's ghost or Pete's.

"Shhhh!" Rain hissed. "Callahan's on deck. . . ."

'Bastian glanced over Rain's head at Charlie, who stared as his friend held a conversation with empty air. Charlie really tried; he concentrated with all his might and squinted in 'Bastian's general direction. But there was nothing there. "Don't worry," 'Bastian said, trying for her sake to "speak" at a lower volume. "I'm pretty sure you're the only one who can see and hear me."

"I guess you're right," she said as she turned back and asked Charlie, "You're not getting any of this, are you?"

Charlie grumbled, "I'm *getting* you to a doctor—as soon as possible."

Charlie watched Rain turn away and say, "Ignore him" to the room. For a second nothing happened, then she struggled to stifle a laugh.

Charlie felt the blood rise in his face, "Hey! What's he saying about me?" And then hearing his own words, he stiffened. *Oh, great. I'm starting to believe this derangement.*

Thunder rumbled in the distance. But the storm had chosen to build rather than approach.

"How is this happening?" Rain asked.

'Bastian shook his head. "I'm not sure. But it has something to do with the snake charm. I seem to be tied to it. I go wherever it goes. And during the day . . . I think I sleep inside it. . . ." He didn't sound too sure.

Unconsciously, Rain's right hand rubbed back and forth along the armband. "What is it?" she asked. "What do you know about it?"

"Not enough." A hundred unhappy memories—everything he had never told Rain about the war and the crash and his old life—flooded over his countenance.

With a clarity as crisp and immediate as the day it happened, he flashed back on the *Island Belle*'s cockpit. The windshield was shattered and the B-17 was quickly filling with water. *We've crashed,* he thought stupidly.

She brought us down, and now we're sinking! He tried to move, but his ankle was trapped between the mangled dash and his seat. Pain from his calf and thigh tore through his brain. His hand came away from them, wet and sticky. And when the cold salt water flowed over his leg and into the wound, he screamed. He tried to regain his senses. *Stay calm! Stay calm! There isn't much time! You can't save your men if you don't save yourself!* He inhaled deeply and dove down beneath the waterline, using both hands to pry his injured leg free. By the time he had won his release, the cockpit was completely submerged. He couldn't breathe. Thoughts of his crewmates had disappeared. *I can't breathe!* He swam out through the broken windshield. His lungs burned. He tried to stay calm, to stay focused, to simply move through the water. *But am I even heading toward the surface?* There was no air left, nothing left. *I'm going to die.*

Rain prompted him: "How long have you had it?"

'Bastian looked at her. His ethereal body took a deep breath that didn't actually draw in any air. "There was this accident," he said.

"I know," she said. "Joe told us."

Joe. Of course. The only one I didn't kill. He nodded. "A rescue boat found me treading water. I was in a pretty bad way." In his mind, the image shifted from the plane to the infirmary at Tío Samuel Naval Base.

Here the memory was less distinct. A room so white, it practically glowed. The walls were white. The sheets were white. The bed was painted white. 'Bastian couldn't focus on anything. The whiteness overwhelmed him, seared him. He was burning up. "I guess I was feverish. I nearly died."

Then two old hands reached toward him. They slipped the snake charm onto his wrist. It felt cool and soothing. *Is it glowing too? Not white, but gold?* He realized he had been thrashing in the white bed only as the thrashing stopped. Only as he finally fell into a deep sleep.

And in the present, woke anew. Old images faded but the old wound still ached. *Can a ghost feel pain? Phantom pain,* he supposed. He looked at his granddaughter. "The charm belonged to *my* grandmother. I had never seen her without it. When I was sick, she put it on my wrist. My *abuela* always said it was her snake charm that healed me. I gave more credit to the doctors. But now . . . well . . ." he finished dryly, "I'm beginning to wonder."

He reached toward Rain's left arm, stopping just short of *not* being able to touch the charm. Rain grinned, practically bouncing on her heels. "I'm just so glad you're back. You are *never* going away again."

He turned so she wouldn't catch his pained expression. "Raindrop . . ." he began, but he was interrupted. By the sudden lack of sound. The engine had stopped.

"What the devil?!" In the forecabin, a confused Callahan stared from the water to the controls and back again. He quickly tested the ignition. Tested it again. "Come on!" Click. Click. Click. It wouldn't turn over.

"Blast!" He slammed his fist against the panel. He crossed the deck through the soft rain and yanked open the hatch to the main cabin, leaping down the steps, not bothering to close the hatch behind him. Without stopping, he proceeded across the empty room.

He didn't notice two sets of eyes peering through the wooden slats of the now-closed closet door. Inside the cramped cabinet, Rain and Charlie tried not to breathe. The handle of the metal detector was pressing into Charlie's back, but he was too scared to move.

Callahan opened the door to the engine room (more like an engine closet, actually), letting a sliver of light into the dark, dank space. He reached forward and pulled a chain that snapped on a free-hanging light-bulb. He didn't see the Eight, standing in a circle around the engine itself, holding their hands over it, willing it to stop. But 'Bastian, standing behind Callahan, did see them. *My boys*, he thought. Then he called out to Rain, "Looks like we've got a little help!" Inside the closet, Rain flinched. She had to remind herself that no one else could hear 'Bastian no matter how loud he yelled.

Callahan took a step forward, walking through a

smoky Bear Mitchell without noticing or stopping. He knelt down beside the engine and spoke to it threateningly, "Now what's your problem?"

'Bastian kept ricocheting back and forth between behaving like the living and enjoying the freedom of a ghost. He moved stealthily to the closet and whispered through the door, as if afraid Callahan might hear. "We've still got to get you two out of here and off this boat." He searched the cabin with his eyes, which lit upon the scuba gear. "That's it. We'll sneak you out under the water. He can't hurt what he can't see."

"Can't see a bloody thing wrong. . . ." Callahan growled. He reached over with a big paw and pulled a rusted toolbox closer. It scraped along the floor, stopping in the middle of Ducky Simpson's foot. Callahan flipped open the lid and fished out a large wrench, which he began to apply to a bolt that held the engine casing in place. Big Harry and Little Harry lowered their hands over the bolt. It wouldn't budge. Callahan shifted his stance to get more leverage, knocking the door partially closed in the process with his butt.

'Bastian saw their chance. "O.K. It's now or never."

Inside the cabinet, Rain reached out to open the door. Charlie grabbed her hand to stop her. *Is she nuts?!* Without speaking, she looked him straight in the eye.

He allowed her to remove his hand from hers. Under her steady, sure gaze, he allowed her to open the door. They slipped out, practically on tiptoe.

Excited and again too loud, 'Bastian spoke: "Grab up the scuba gear." It so startled Rain, she nearly tripped back into Charlie. This time *he* steadied *her*.

'Bastian pointed toward the semi-closed door to the engine room: "Careful, he's right in there." Rain gave her grandfather a look and reached out both hands in a gesture that clearly indicated she was ready to strangle him right about now. Then she turned to Charlie and pointed toward the scuba gear.

But Charlie was too stressed to focus. He held out his hands helplessly, not getting her drift at all. Rain took his arm and guided him over to the gear. They took the bare minimum. Both slipped on masks and grabbed up flippers. Rain carefully hefted an air tank onto her back. It was awkward going. Charlie cradled his air tank in his arms, then impulsively reached for an underwater flashlight. The air tank slipped from his grip. He fumbled for it desperately and just managed to catch it painfully on his foot. A panicked Rain reached over, steadying the air tank with one hand and slapping another over Charlie's mouth, muffling his cry.

But not enough. Callahan froze at the sound. He re-gripped the wrench like a weapon and turned toward the door. Slowly, he pulled it open and peered into the main cabin. There was no one there.

No one in his view at least. Rain and Charlie were pressed flat as possible against the common wall that the cabin shared with the engine room. They were closer to Callahan than the engine itself, but they were just out of his line of vision. For a tense beat, none of the players, including the invisible 'Bastian, moved. Finally, slowly, Callahan turned back toward the engine—though he was careful not to let the door close again.

Once again, Callahan applied the wrench to the bolt. The wrench slipped and smashed his thumb against the engine's metal casing. He inhaled through his teeth, then shouted, "Blast!" Furious and frustrated, he began slamming the wrench against the bolt over and over. "Blast! Blast! Blast! Blast! Blast!!"

'Bastian saw that the man was fully focused on his outburst. This time the new-minted ghost managed to keep his mouth shut and simply signaled Rain to move with a wave.

Rain turned her head to Charlie and jerked it toward the open hatch. Then she led the way out, under the cover of Callahan's still banging wrench. It was still hard to move quietly with all they were carrying, but somehow they managed.

'Bastian stayed behind to keep an eye on Callahan. Or at least he tried. Without warning, he was suddenly pulled backward toward the hatch by the power of the snake charm. Embarrassed, he tried to recover his dignity as he was tugged along, unconsciously checking to see if his old crew had noticed. Then he raced after the others, running up the steps as if he were alive.

It was still raining softly on deck, but the sea was quiet and the fog had lifted for the moment. The storm remained a distant threat, as if waiting for her moment.

Rain and Charlie looked out toward Tío Samuel—not too far away across the water. They put on their flippers in silence. Charlie picked their shoes up off the deck. Then with a resigned shrug, he dropped them into the ocean one by one.

'Bastian slid up to Rain. He whispered, "Slip into the water. When you get far enough away so that he can't hear you, ditch the tanks." He pointed to the island. "It'll be a swim to Tío Samuel, but I've seen both of you handle tougher. Miller's there."

Rain stopped him, whispering, "He is?"

"He has a job as a night janitor."

"How do you know that? Is it a ghost thing?"

He frowned. "I know nothing about ghost things. Wish I did. Too new at it I guess. No, Miller got the job two weeks ago when your dad couldn't use him on the boat. Navy gives him free room and board, plus days and weekends off for surfing Tío Sam's beaches, which are off-limits otherwise. He was bragging about the waves last time I saw him."

An anxious Charlie grabbed Rain's arm. "What's going on?"

'Bastian returned to his main point: "Miller can get you back to San Próspero." He smiled nervously and pointed at the snake charm. "And I'll be with you the whole way."

She smiled and turned to Charlie, pointing toward Tío Sam's. He nodded confirmation. They both turned to climb down off the boat. Unfortunately, they turned in opposite directions, and their air tanks collided with a very loud CLANK! They froze, as the metallic sound echoed across the water. Slowly, all three of them looked toward the open hatch. . . .

Belowdecks, the clank still echoed. Callahan wasted no time. Gripping the wrench, he leapt to his feet and ran out into the main cabin through Bear, who seemed to take no more notice of Callahan than Callahan did of him.

Scooping up the harpoon gun with his free hand, Callahan raced toward the hatch. He ducked his head like a bull, then charged out onto the deck in time to see the two kids fall backward into the water. Without hesitation, he dived in after them, fully clothed and well armed.

Rain and Charlie were already swimming away, side by side through the dark silent water. Charlie clicked on the flashlight and swam unawares toward the semitransparent, softly glowing apparition that gently bobbed up and down in the sea. But Rain saw him. The Dark Man, her grandfather, young and handsome and "rakish." He was completely submerged but dry by all appearances, still dressed in his bomber jacket and standing upright, as if on some nonexistent nodding plateau. He pointed back over her shoulder, and his voice—unaffected by being underwater—rang in her mind: "Look out!"

Rain turned in time to see Callahan take aim with the harpoon gun. She tried to move. He pulled the trigger.

CHAPTER FIFTEEN

HEALER

Rain was still flailing to get out of the way when she felt the harpoon tear across her skin. She screamed through her regulator as the pain burned from her left arm up into her brain. Charlie yelled too. He reached toward Rain, unsure of how to help. The harpoon had grazed her below the shoulder, and the flashlight revealed the dark red discoloration of her own blood in the surrounding water. Then something slightly lower caught her eye. One of the gold snakes on the armband was beginning to glow, and both Rain and Charlie could feel more than hear a distinct hum in the water, like an electrical charge building. Rain saw the golden glow move rapidly up her arm to her new wound. The glow engulfed the wound and plunged inside it. Just as quickly, the gleam faded—leaving her completely healed.

Rain and Charlie had barely an instant to stare at each other through their masks. Charlie hadn't seen any glow, but when he'd seen her arm heal—the wound vanishing before his eyes—he nearly swallowed his own regulator. To Rain, the glow had felt warm and wonderful; her pain was gone.

But Callahan wasn't. He hadn't reloaded, didn't have a second harpoon, so he released the gun and swam toward them, brandishing the steel wrench. His massive legs propelled him rapidly through the water, despite the long khakis he wore and his lack of flippers.

'Bastian, furious that this monster would fire on his Rain, moved to intercept, yelling, "Why don't you pick on someone your own size?!" He took a useless swing at Callahan, but of course his ethereal fist passed right through its solid target. Unaware of his ghostly opponent, Callahan swam through 'Bastian toward the kids. He was almost on top of Rain, who remained stunned and focused on her healed limb. A desperate Charlie rolled back in the water and kicked Callahan with his flippered feet. But kicking Callahan was like kicking a block of granite. Charlie's heroism delayed their foe for mere seconds, and the kick pushed Charlie farther from Rain than Callahan was.

But it snapped Rain out of her stupor. Seeing a slim chance, she lunged for the wrench and managed to snatch it out of Callahan's distracted grip. Instead, he grabbed her wrist; he held it tight, shaking it. In pain again, she dropped the wrench, which sank out of our lives for a good long while.

Rain struggled in his grasp, but he pulled her toward him by her wrist, and when she got in close, he yanked the regulator right out of her mouth and stuck it in his own. He took a deep breath, while her continued efforts to escape robbed her of what little air remained in her lungs. He began to swim them both to the surface, and though she fought to be free of him, she didn't fight the upward momentum. She needed air, and she needed it fast. Charlie followed, kicking furiously. 'Bastian rose, pulled by the snake charm and his own desire.

Callahan and Rain broke the surface together. Still locked in his grip, she gasped for air. He spit out her regulator. They were about a dozen yards from the boat. The sky maintained a fine but insistent rain.

"Let go of me!" she yelled, struggling.

"Forget it, girlie!" His jackknife was suddenly out and open in his free hand: a game of *Attack of the Killer Tourists* played for keeps.

Charlie emerged a few feet away. But before he could do anything (assuming there was anything he *could* do), all three living players turned their heads toward the sound of the *Bootstrap*'s restarting engines. The Eight were gone from the cabin cruiser. Whatever ghostly power they had exerted upon the engine to keep it from turning over had evaporated with them. The cruiser began to slowly pull away from the swimmers.

"My boat!" Callahan took less than a second to register his new dilemma, before releasing Rain with a growl and swimming for all he was worth after the *Bootstrap*. It was a Herculean effort. I'd call it admirable, had it been achieved by a man whose scent I liked even slightly better. Callahan just managed to intercept the cruiser, making a desperate grab for the diver's ladder and snagging it. Soaking wet, he pulled himself up onto the deck. Then, scanning back and forth for further intruders, he ran to the forecabin, reached in with his long gorilla-esque arm and shut off the engine once more.

Then he was at the bow, snapping on a blinding spotlight and turning it on the dark water for some sign of the two kids. But they had gone back under, out of sight. Dripping and frustrated, he muttered under his breath, "Could be anywhere . . ." And then it hit him. The first sign that the man knew fear: "The *zemi!*"

Moments later, he was back in the main cabin, beelining for his duffel. He crouched down, grabbed it up and stuck his hand in, groping blindly. "Come on . . . Come on . . ." He felt something hard and cold and metal. His expression changed from desperation to hope. Slowly, he removed it from the bag and held it up to his face. The faux armband glistened under the overhead light. "Yes!"

He sat back on his haunches, relieved and blissfully unaware that Rain had pulled a double switch. Water trickled down his cheek from his flattened blond hair, and he rubbed it away with the side of a thick and equally wet arm. Not without satisfaction, he thought of Rain. *Stupid brat. Got away, but didn't get the* zemi. His face contorted into a legitimately evil grin, and he spoke aloud, "S'alright. Have another chance at you, kid. Lay odds I will."

Scant minutes later, Callahan was back in the forecabin. The engine restarted with ease, and he piloted her off toward his rendezvous.

'Bastian's softly glowing head stuck up out of the water, watching as the boat pulled away and quickly disappeared from sight. Small crests of waves flowed right through him, which was more than mildly disconcerting. He shook it off and allowed himself to sink, to submerge.

He floated straight down, still in a standing position, arms folded across his chest. Rain and Charlie hung in the water, waiting. Charlie had the flashlight trained on her arm, looking for a harpoon wound that no longer existed. Rain, who imagined with disgust that she could taste Callahan's foul mouth on her regulator, was focused upward, watching 'Bastian descend, so she didn't see what her grandfather saw. His men, his crew, staggered below the two kids like a glowing trail of bread crumbs. Leading down, down toward the dark ocean floor.

As he leveled off beside Rain, his sad face grew determined. He spoke evenly: "The coast is clear. You can ditch the tanks and swim for Tío Sam's."

Rain nodded, tugging at Charlie and pointing toward the surface. Charlie kicked upward.

"But . . ." said 'Bastian. Rain grabbed Charlie, stopping him. She turned to face her grandfather, who quietly said, ". . . I can't go with you." Bewildered, Rain stared at him through her mask.

He pointed down toward his former comrades. Their need carried through the water into Rain and 'Bastian's minds. "Captain, please . . . The mission . . . Send us home . . . home . . ." She stared at the Eight. Their voices had grown more insistent and crisp, like 'Bastian's. Less like liquid and smoke. *It's the snake charm*, she realized. With it, she could hear them as clearly as the living. Without it, she needed to be in direct contact with their essence, and even then they'd sound distant, like whispers. *But I could see them. I could hear them. Even without the charm! WHY? Charlie can't! Callahan couldn't! Just . . . me . . .*

'Bastian brought her back to the matter at hand: "They need me to finish the mission, so they can finally go home." Her eyes snapped up to meet his. He sighed. "Rain, they've waited so long . . ."

She shook her head vehemently! Then she pointed to the armband, turned to Charlie and practically pulled her friend toward the surface. 'Bastian tried not to follow. He tried concentrating on the mission, on the men. But the connection to the snake charm was too strong, and he began to rise against his will. Below him, he watched his crew start to dim and fade away.

For the second time, Rain and Charlie broke the surface. The rain was sharp and stinging; the seas, just beginning to chop. Treading water, they removed their regulators.

"What's going on?" Charlie asked.

" 'Bastian's trying to ditch me!"

"Rain . . ." Charlie sounded dubious. But whether of the ghost's intentions or its mere existence was unclear.

"I am not trying to ditch you, young lady." 'Bastian had surfaced beside his granddaughter. He was as determined as ever to rescue his men. "I have to help them find peace. It must be why I'm still hanging around."

"No!" Rain was equally determined. "You're here to be with me! I don't *want* you finishing any missions."

"We're right above the wreck. I can sense it somehow. That's why they stopped the boat here." He pointed at the snake charm, knowing she knew what he wanted, what he needed.

"No, no, NO!!"

"No, what?!" Charlie demanded.

Rain ignored him, yelling at no one: "I won't lose you again!"

Charlie muttered, "Can't believe I'm a third wheel in a crowd of two."

'Bastian leaned in, quiet and serious. "Raindrop. This is important."

Rain looked away. Torn and torn up. She couldn't bear it if he left again. *I just got him back* . . . She snuck another look. At this face she barely recognized. Her grandfather before he was her grandfather. When he had other, larger, priorities. *I can't lose him again.* . . . For a long moment of quiet rain and less-than-gentle up-and-down ocean flow, she said nothing. *But if I keep him like this* . . . Finally, she turned and said, "Charlie, we're gonna dive down and find that B-17."

"What?!" Charlie yelled.

'Bastian was equally shocked. "You don't have to do that."

"The snake charm heals," she said, trying to convince herself as much as anyone. "And these ghosts have been hurting for a long time. I have to see this through even if it means losing you."

"Thanks, you're so kind," said Charlie, who thought she was speaking to him.

"Maybe that's how you become part of something larger than yourself—by doing something . . ." She cringed. ". . . Unselfish."

'Bastian beamed at her proudly, but he still didn't want her at risk. "Just drop the thing. If it sinks straight down, it'll fall close enough."

"And let it land fifty feet from the plane, stranding you at the bottom of the ocean for eternity? I don't think so."

Charlie had had enough. He was trying desperately to hold on to the safe normal world he knew. "Rain, you can't possibly believe all this stuff!"

"You saw how it healed my arm. Are you telling me you *don't* believe?"

"I'm sure not admitting I *do!*" He glowered at her for a good five seconds, then relented. "All right, let's go."

She smiled. The kids replaced their regulators. Then all three dove back down under the surface of the water.

Rain and 'Bastian followed the glowing bread-crumb trail of ghosts down toward the ocean floor. Charlie followed Rain, shining the flashlight rapidly back and forth. By this time, he wanted to find the plane as much as his friend. Find it and get out of there. *If I live through this, my mom is gonna kill me.*

Rain could hear the drums in her head. The farther down they searched, the more insistent the rhythm. Another smile crept onto her face. *When did this become fun?* There was no sign of the *Belle*. The temperature of the water decreased steadily as they descended. Rain and Charlie were both wearing T-shirts and shorts and wishing for wet suits.

'Bastian pointed past a coral reef. Rain swam over it. Charlie followed. Beyond the reef, their objective: a shadow that seemed to drain away all surrounding light. Charlie swept his flashlight across the dark shape. The *Island Belle* had seen better decades. It lay wrecked, rusted, seaweed-covered and decidedly ominous at the bottom of the sea.

Charlie felt his heart racing; he was scared, but despite himself, he was curious now too. He and Rain exchanged a glance, then swam toward the B-17.

They swam along the fuselage until they found a hatch. Rain tried to pull it open, but the rusted handle snapped off in her hands. Charlie tapped her on the shoulder and pointed.

There was a large open crack in the fuselage about

three feet away. Large enough to swim through. Rain paused. Then swam into the plane. Charlie followed. Drums, heartbeats, whatever they were, were loud in both their ears.

Carefully, they swam through the *Belle*'s cramped interior toward her cockpit. Charlie held the light steady. As they entered the radio room, their movement spooked a small shark, which fled, churning up a cloud of silty muck. The light danced among the silt, revealing nothing. They swam through the cloud and found themselves face-to-face with a grinning skull.

Both kids let out frightened squeals through their regulators. They grabbed each other's arms to steady their nerves. Rain moved closer. The skull topped a skeleton dressed in tattered World War II garb. Charlie's light soon found a second skeleton and a third. Rain stared at the first skull, trying to see the face that used to surround it. But she didn't recognize him. Didn't recognize any of them. *Dead people all look alike to me.* The light slid past the name tag on his uniform: "Grier." *It's Pete,* she thought. *This was Pete.* Now she knew she was doing the right thing.

Charlie wasn't so sure. He didn't know what they were supposed to do in here, down here. But whatever it was, it was past time they got it done and got out. He found Rain's eyes and pleaded to her with his own. She nodded and led him around the remains of Pete Grier and into the cockpit.

Rain entered the small space, followed by Charlie. His light found another skeleton wearing a bomber jacket and leather helmet, sitting in the copilot's seat. Charlie shrugged at Rain. *Now what?*

On Rain's armband, the snake that had healed her flashed gold once again. 'Bastian materialized from the snake charm, facing away from them. He was still glowing softly but no longer transparent. As his glow changed from white to gold, he looked almost solid enough to touch. But Rain's hand still went right through his back, and she quickly pulled away. He ignored or didn't feel the intrusion. He took his seat. The pilot's seat. He said, "All right, boys, prepare for takeoff."

"Roger that."

Rain locked her hands around Charlie's arm—tight enough to make him wince. Tom McMinn's glowing spirit had materialized around his skeleton—solid enough to render the bones within invisible.

"Finally." This voice came from behind. Rain turned just in time to see Pete's spirit looming in the hatchway, superimposed over his skeleton, too. Pete smiled, but not at her. She wasn't sure if the crew were even aware of their presence.

Tom spoke into a radio whose frayed wires no longer led anywhere: "Call in."

In the nose, Bear and Billy found their bones and checked in with their commanding officers. "Navigator, ready." "Bombardier, checking in."

Back in the radio room, the two skeletons Pete had left behind came to life as Lance and Ducky. "Radio operator, checking in." "Ball turret, checking in."

Behind them, Big Harry and Little Harry were also ready. "Left waist gunner." "Right waist gunner."

Rain was dedicating a lot of energy to remembering to breathe. 'Bastian began flipping switches on his control panel. His glow infected everything he touched, and that glow was spreading like wildfire throughout the *Belle*, inside and out. Soon the entire wreck was surrounded by an electric golden aura.

'Bastian paused. "Top turret?"

"Right behind you, Cap," Pete said cheerfully.

"Tail gunner?"

"Still goldbricking." Tommy laughed. "Hit that son in the head once, and he'll milk it for weeks."

"That's right. Poor kid." And for half a second, Rain felt bad for Old Joe, missing the mission one more time.

'Bastian set back to work. "Let's run the checklist, Lieutenant. Generators?"

Tommy stopped him. "Captain Bohique, I can

pretty much guarantee that nothing is working on this bird."

And Pete: "He's right, Cap. You think too much about it, we ain't never gettin' home."

The Dark Man nodded. "All right, then, just start the engines for me."

"Roger that."

One engine no longer had a propeller, but the golden aura flashed around the other three and the bent and rusted props began to turn, churning up the water and muck.

Rain glanced at Charlie, wondering what he saw. Wondering whether he'd believe her when she told him what *she* saw.

Charlie's eyes were wide. He was glad for Rain's grip on his arm, because the pain gave him something to focus on and kept him from screaming. He saw no glow. No gold aura around the B-17. And the pilot seat seemed empty. But his flashlight was locked on the copilot's bones, which were actively flipping switches on the busted control panel. And worse yet—out of the corner of his eye, because he *would NOT* turn around— Charlie could just see the skeleton from the radio room, grinning over his shoulder. *It followed us to the cockpit! It got up and followed us! That can't be good!*

'Bastian remained in the moment. If he was aware of

Rain and Charlie at all, he didn't let on. Rain watched him turn to Tommy, give his lieutenant a wink, and say, "Let's go home." Then he pushed on the throttle, and the bomber abruptly lurched forward. Rain and Charlie exchanged yet another glance before grabbing hold of the seats in front of them. And just in time. Because the *Island Belle* was ready for takeoff.

CHAPTER SIXTEEN

THE FINAL FLIGHT OF THE ISLAND BELLE

Rain and Charlie felt the *Belle* lurch forward again.

"Our girl's a little sluggish tonight," 'Bastian said lovingly. He eased the throttle once more, and the bomber began to move in earnest. Which was interesting, because her landing gear wasn't down. The glowing rusted hulk was just taxiing on its belly through the sand. But it was picking up speed.

A current of water surged in through the shattered windshield and out of the cockpit past Rain, Charlie and Pete. The kids dug their hands into the torn fabric and rotted padding of 'Bastian and Tommy's seats, until they found the metal framework beneath and something real to hold on to against the flow. Charlie finally got brave enough to sneak a peek behind and saw Pete's bony hands brace his skeleton in the hatch. Charlie had a not-so-sudden desperate impulse to flee. *But I'm not going out that way!*

The B-17 was really starting to move now. 'Bastian pulled back on the wheel. "That's my girl," he said. And *Belle* responded. She began to lift up off the ocean floor. Bouncing once, twice, gaining altitude—even if she was still below sea level.

Looking terrified and amazed at the same time, Charlie and Rain held on tighter still, bracing themselves against the bumpy "takeoff."

Finally, the *Belle* left her silty runway and was legitimately up and "flying" through the ocean. 'Bastian pulled back some more, and she continued to rise at a steeper angle. Rain and Charlie quickly adjusted their stances to keep from sliding back as the bomber climbed for the surface.

From the nose, Bear spoke to 'Bastian, via some kind of spook-wave radio system: "Need me to set a course, Cap?"

"No thanks, Lieutenant. We're mighty close to home. I know where we're goin'."

Above the water line, the rain continued to softly replenish the calm and peaceful sea. Then—*whoosh*— the glowing B-17 broke the surface and continued its ascent into the sky. This gold-glowing, blushing *Belle* was like a new-made bride, with a train of seaweed and salt water trailing behind her. And this particular bride had a bridesmaid too: a storm head was building in her wake.

Inside the cockpit, the water rapidly began to drain away. 'Bastian, Tommy and Pete took no notice. But Rain and Charlie did. They were still holding on for dear life, but when the water fell below neck level, both kids spit out their regulators to shout over the wind that was now blasting through the nonexistent windshield.

Dripping and shivering, an excited Rain was wearing a big old grin: "Now, do you believe?!"

Charlie looked around, stunned. He saw no ghosts. But there was a fully animated skeleton sitting right in front of him and another standing right behind him. *And the thing does seem to be flying. . . .* He turned back to Rain and shouted, "Let's just say I'm keeping an open mind!"

The *Belle* rattled and shook. And shook again. And

shook more violently. Tommy turned to 'Bastian: "She's building, Captain. She's on our tail."

"Who?" Bastian asked.

"Julia."

"Who?"

"Hurricane Julia. She's back. To finish what she started. To make sure we never complete the mission. Never get home. She took us out once, and she doesn't want her works thwarted now. She doesn't want us to get away. And she's back to get the last of us. She's back for you, Cap."

More drums. Rain and 'Bastian both looked outside with new eyes. The clouds were already black, yet somehow getting blacker. Lightning flashed all around with less than a "one-one-thousand" before the thunder followed. The B-17 was rocked. Thrown down, then up. The wind sheared across her. And it didn't take ghost senses for Charlie to hear the pieces of its fuselage grinding and tearing apart. The aura was holding the bird together, but every magick has its limit.

More lightning and thunder struck—even closer and now in perfect synch. And in that half a second between the blinding flash and the darkness that followed, Rain and 'Bastian both saw her: a figure of cloud and wind and rain and flashing eyes: Hurricane Julia herself.

The Dark Man's expression hardened into a dangerous grin. "So we have an enemy," he said, holding a hand up to his neck to speak into the approximate location of where his radio microphone should have been. "That's something this crew knows how to handle. Battle stations, boys."

Rain looked back over her shoulder. Pete was gone from the hatchway, but she heard his voice saying: "Roger that, Captain. Top turret ready."

This was instantly followed by four other voices, announcing that bombardier, left waist gunner, right waist gunner and ball turret were in position and prepared for a fight.

But 'Bastian groused: "No tail gunner. Flank's exposed."

And that's when the *second* snake on Rain's armband made its presence felt. The first was still glowing gold, maintaining the healing aura that had resurrected the *Belle.* But Rain felt a charge and looked down. The other snake was glowing now too: a bright electric blue. It was powerful, mesmerizing, and it seemed to speak to her deep beneath the conscious level of her brain. Suddenly, she knew what she had to do. "C'mon," she said to Charlie.

"What?! Where?!"

She didn't answer, couldn't explain. But she climbed

through the hatch, and Charlie followed without argument. *After all that's happened so far, what's the* point *of arguing?*

They stripped off what remained of their scuba gear and, barefooted, made their way back through the B-17, passing the ghosts—or as Charlie saw them, the animated skeletons—of Lance and the two Harrys at their posts. There were holes in *Belle*'s skin large enough to drop them to their deaths, but they managed to avoid them and finally reached the tail gun.

And just in time—lightning flashed again, revealing Julia, now bigger than ten *Island Belle*s, reaching a giant hand of cloud and wind and rain and lightning toward the exposed rear of the bomber. She grasped and just missed—the old bomber was just barely out of reach—but the B-17 rocked and bucked, plummeted and rose like a mad bull.

Rain slipped into the ragged, rotting seat that once belonged to Tail Gunner Joey. She tried to aim the large gun, but it was frozen in place by decades of rust. She turned to Charlie. "Help me!" He slid in beside her, the skinny teenage boy sharing the man-sized seat with his equally skinny best friend. No longer asking for explanations, Charlie helped Rain wrench the gun out of its locked state. Something cracked audibly, and the thing moved, nearly slipping off its housing completely—but the gold aura held it more-or-less in place for Rain.

She watched then as the second snake's electric blue flared on her arm and from within the gun itself. She knew she was locked and loaded. "Where's the trigger?" she shouted.

"Here!" He guided her hand. *All those video games were finally paying off.* . . .

She waited for the next lightning strike—and didn't have long to wait. There was Julia, her dark cloud mane streaming around her, her eyes flashing with electricity—and her expression: pure fury. But Rain was angry too. This woman—this thing—had tried to kill her grandfather twice. *Once after he was already dead!* Rain rotated the gun, taking aim. Charlie's hand still surrounded hers on the trigger. And when the lightning flashed again, she opened fire.

Streaks of electric blue sailed from the tail gun's muzzle. They lit up the sky (for Rain, not Charlie) and struck the female fury right between the eyes. Rain could hear the storm shriek. Even Charlie heard a cry on the wind that sounded almost human, something very angry and in pain.

"She's hit!" Rain shouted. Charlie didn't ask who "she" was. From his point of view, Rain had aimed the gun toward the darkest section of the storm. He saw no "she"—but he saw the locus of darkness moving. Without thinking—for once—he wrenched the big gun around to keep it on target.

Rain didn't think to ask how her friend knew which way to aim. She fired again. The blue light seared across the sky and struck the spirit—the *goddess*—of the storm once more. Rain could see her shrinking under the blue fire. And Charlie could now see gaps in the cloud cover, exposing a few stars.

But the darkest of the dark clouds moved again, and Charlie followed it with the gun, while Rain maintained fire. And she wasn't the only one. From both the top turret and the ball turret, Pete and Ducky fired more streaks of blue light back on the enemy as well. For the third time in four nights, the drums in Rain's brain rose to a crescendo. The shrieking continued, louder and more horrible, but Rain and the others were merciless. The blue fire strafed the clouds . . . until Hurricane Julia finally gave up the ghost. Or at least the *Belle*.

Pete's voice crackled in Rain's ear: "Well, we didn't get the kill. But we sent her scurryin', Captain. I think we're home free."

Rain remembered to breathe. The drums were silent, but she was sure she could hear an orchestra of strings hailing their triumph. She released the gun.

Charlie did the same. They looked each other in the eye intensely. Then embarrassed, they both looked away.

Two minutes later, they were back in the cockpit and once again gripping the back of Tommy and 'Bastian's seats for dear life. For a second, it had felt like it was all over. Then they remembered just where they were and how precarious their situation remained.

'Bastian again spoke into his "radio": "Sergeant Pedros."

"Yes, Captain."

"Let 'em know we're coming."

"Roger that." And at his station, Lance spoke into his ancient, rusted, waterlogged unit. It glowed a beautiful gold. "Tío Samuel, this is Broadway-Niner-Niner-Four requesting permission for an emergency landing."

The tower at Tío Sam's airfield was painted white, like most of the base. Inside, Ensign Chris LeVell, a confused young air traffic controller, was sitting in front of his radar screen trying to identify the source of the strange broadcast. "Please, repeat designation. Acknowledge."

Lance Pedros' voice crackled in Ensign LeVell's ears. "Roger. That's Broadway-Niner-Niner-Four requesting permission to land."

Commander Stevens wasn't supposed to be there that night. He had just been in the mood for a walk in the rain, and his feet had found their way to the tower without any help. Now he leaned in over LeVell's shoulder. "What did he say? Put him on speaker."

LeVell flinched, suddenly realizing who was behind him. Then he nodded and said, "Yes, sir."

On the *Belle,* Lance's ghost was shaking his head and smiling. "Captain, what we have here is a failure to communicate."

The Dark Man grinned. "Patch me through."

"Roger that. You tell 'em, Cap."

'Bastian took a deep breath, then: "Tío Samuel Naval Base, this is Broadway-Niner-Niner-Four. We're flying on three engines and a prayer here. I'm requesting permission to land, but I'm landing with or without it."

Stevens leaned in closer, hovering over LeVell's mic, listening to that strange, distant voice. "Broadway? That's a B-17 designation. No one's used that for fifty years."

"Well, we are running a bit behind schedule."

Pete, back in position in the hatchway, chuckled. "You ain't just whistlin' Dixie, Captain."

'Bastian, Tommy and Rain laughed. Charlie yelled, "What? What's so funny?"

In the tower, Stevens' first instinct was to mobilize. Something on the scope was coming in under his watch, and the thought of a terrorist attack was never far from any military man's mind. But Tío Sam's held no strategic importance and had never been considered a likely target. The truth was, the base had been caught flat-out unprepared. By the time Stevens got any birds in the air, whatever was coming would already be here. All he could do was press a button, lean in and order Broadway-Niner-Niner-Four to circle. Then he shut off the microphone, pressed another button and put the entire base on alert.

But Captain Sebastian Bohique was tired of waiting for some swabbie's approval. Still smiling, he pushed forward on the wheel. And the *Belle* began her descent.

'Bastian eased up on the throttle. "Lower landing gear."

"Roger," Tom said, flipping another switch.

The golden glow prodded the landing gear bays open. But the glow could only do so much. The bay doors jammed long before opening wide enough for the rotted rubber wheels to lower. The gear was stuck and—glow or no glow—wasn't budging.

Tommy turned to 'Bastian, shrugged and drolly commented, "Could be a rough landing."

The *Island Belle* continued her descent, entering a mild fog bank that shrouded Tío Sam's. Through the shattered windshield, Rain could now see the runway lights shimmering hazily in the mist. *We're going to land! We're really going to land!* She turned to Charlie and shouted, "Hold on!"

He rolled his eyes and yelled, "You think?!"

'Bastian said, "Crew, assume positions for crash landing."

Rain shouted, "Crash?!"

And Charlie yelled, "WHAT?!"

But they didn't crash. The *Belle* came in for a landing. Her aura acted as something of a cushion—though the fuselage still scraped and sparked against the tarmac, throwing off magickal golden flashes and not-so-magickal red-hot fragments of metal. Inside the cockpit, Charlie was fairly certain he'd be one with Rain's ghost crew soon enough. He and Rain were barely able to hold on to the seats and each other as the bomber shook and jumped.

Ghost or no ghost, 'Bastian was rattled by *Belle*'s quaking hull and his inability to without wheels, bring her to a halt. He was afraid she'd break apart. Afraid that if she did, if she broke or blew, the mission would still end in failure. His men would still be lost. *And Rain?!* For the first time since resuming command, he turned around and saw his granddaughter and her friend. *My God, what have I done?!*

He tried to smile at her, tried to reassure her. "Smooth as silk, huh?" She forced a smile back at him.

And just then, finally, the bomber skidded to a full stop.

Rain and Charlie were still vibrating. But they wore the kind of goofy grins that only come with knowing you lived through something you had no right to.

Rain scanned the cockpit. The golden aura was fading. And so was the flight crew. 'Bastian was again transparent. Rain took note, and her grin faded as quickly as their glow.

'Bastian stood and glanced from Tommy to Pete. "Mission accomplished. We're home."

Still in his seat, Tommy's spirit no longer fully concealed his nodding skull. "Roger that, Captain."

From throughout the plane, the voices flooded Rain and 'Bastian's minds one last time. "Nice flying, Cap." "Knew you could do it." "Better late than never."

"And thanks," Pete said. "Thank you." And on that heartfelt note, his spirit completely faded away along with the last of the *Belle*'s glow. His skeleton collapsed in the hatchway, causing Charlie to jump. Tom's skeleton sat back in its copilot's seat, finally at rest. The Eight were gone, leaving only their bones and tattered clothes, the rusted hulk of the *Island Belle*, Rain, Charlie . . . and 'Bastian.

'Bastian faced his granddaughter, both of them starting to tear up. "I guess I'm next," he said.

"I'm going to miss you so much."

"Same here, Raindrop. But I'm glad we had a chance to say good-bye." He looked away. He wanted to hold her, comfort her, but the Dark Man knew he could not. *Better to make a clean break.* "Now you climb out of here, before the whole thing collapses."

Rain nodded once and then fled; she needed to get out before *she* collapsed. She climbed over the skeleton in the hatchway. Charlie swallowed hard and followed.

They quickly found a large hole in the *Belle* near the nose. They swung down, hanging there, giving each other nods of encouragement, before dropping a few feet to the fog-shrouded pavement below. They could already hear sirens in the distance. As one, they ran across the tarmac in their wet clothes and bare feet and lost themselves in the mist and the brush beside the runway. A strong scent of mint leaves, mixed with ocean salt, surrounded them and seemed to momentarily offer a cocoon of protection from the approaching authorities.

A fine rain was still falling, but Charlie was pretty sure those were tears on Rain's cheeks. Gently, he asked, "Are they all gone?"

Rain looked around. No ghosts. No 'Bastian. "I guess so," she said. "I guess they're at peace now."

"You'd think so, wouldn't you?" Rain wheeled about to find the Dark Man standing behind her, young, handsome, transparent and glowing softly white.

"Papa!"

A smiling 'Bastian shrugged and pointed at Rain's snake charm. "I must still have a mission left to complete."

"Don't make me pretend I'm sorry."

"I won't . . . if you won't."

Charlie watched Rain stare happily at empty space. "Is he still here?"

"Yes!"

"No offense, but . . . why?"

'Bastian considered Charlie's question as the siren's wail heralded the shining headlights of a Navy emergency truck—the first of several vehicles approaching rapidly from down the tarmac. "The snake charm just won't let me go."

Rain asked, "Did your grandmother tell you anything else about it?"

Thinking on that, 'Bastian rubbed his hand over his chin and was distracted by the odd lack of sensation. He couldn't put his hand through his face, and yet there was no true solidity to either part of his body. Like oil and water, they simply wouldn't mix. Recovering his

train of thought, he said, "No . . . but after I was released from the infirmary here, she did take me someplace. She made a point of taking me someplace."

"Then I think you'd better take us too . . ."

The truck pulled to a stop a few yards from the plane.
Its siren abruptly cut out. Rain and Charlie ducked farther down behind the brush and the scent of mint. 'Bastian whispered a "let's get out of here" to Rain. She
tugged on Charlie's arm, and the three of them slinked
away.

No one saw the two teens—let alone the ghost—
thanks to the fog and the GIANT DISTRACTION
parked on the runway. Through the truck's windshield,
two Shore patrolmen looked up at the *Belle* in a state of
pure shock. *This wreck couldn't have landed here. Could
hardly have been towed here in one piece.*

The passenger-side door opened, and Commander
Stevens slowly exited the vehicle. *How in heaven . . . ?*
His eyes gradually took in the entirety of the rusted
hulk of the B-17 that loomed above him, still dripping
salt water and seaweed. An awed whisper escaped his
lips: "Broadway-Niner-Niner-Four . . ."

CHAPTER SEVENTEEN

RENDEZVOUS

Getting back to San Próspero proved far easier than they could have dreamed. 'Bastian knew Tío Sam both from the war and from the occasional Veteran's Day ceremony. He was able to lead them through the base and act as an invisible advance scout to help them avoid the assorted naval personnel running about in semi-urgency. Too, the universe seemed to be cooperating, as the light mist quickly became a dense fog to further cover their movements.

They found Miller mopping up the mess hall alone. He gaped as they approached like two scared drowned rats. "Dudes, what are you doing here?"

"Long story," Rain said. (And the trouble-prone

Miller nodded as if that was explanation enough.) "Can you help us get home?"

And Miller did. He wasn't exactly a brilliant strategist, but again the cards seemed to fall in their favor. The fog helped. So did the fact that this particular Sunday had been Visiting Day on Tío Sam's. Families of various sailors, who didn't have more than a billet for housing on the base, were already scheduled to head back to the big island on a Navy shuttle. A shuttle piloted by Ensign Dusanek, one of Miller's surfing buddies. Miller explained that his two young friends had lost their I.D. badges in the surf, and Dusanek agreed to sneak them on board—an unusually easy prospect as shore patrolmen had been pulled off their regular duty to help investigate the mysterious appearance of a certain skeleton-filled B-17 bomber and the very modern scuba gear found inside. No one, certainly not Dusanek, suspected two thirteen-year-olds could have been behind it.

Before Dusanek led them off, Rain gave Miller a quick hug. "Thanks, Miller. We definitely owe you one."

Miller's smiling head bobbed. "Cool."

Once aboard the shuttle, Rain and Charlie (and an invisible 'Bastian) stuck close to a mom and her two young children. The mom smiled at the teens and wondered if they were traveling alone—and why they had no shoes—but to everyone else it looked as if they were under her supervision. The voyage home was uneventful.

At the docks, where the fog had lifted but the rain persisted, a sailor was collecting I.D. badges from each passenger as he or she debarked. As prearranged, Rain and Charlie waved across the boat to Dusanek and told the sailor that they had already given their badges to the ensign. Dusanek waved back, and the sailor let them pass. Later, if asked, Dusanek would claim he had no idea who those kids were: They waved, so he waved back. That was the plan, anyway. In fact, Dusanek was never asked. Nevertheless, Miller would now owe *him* one.

Ashore, Charlie tugged his damp T-shirt away from his slim chest and said, "It's getting late."

Rain said, "If it weren't raining, we'd be at the party, and there's no way our parents would expect us home by now."

"But it *is* raining."

"You're not really going to cut out?"

"I just said, it's late. I didn't say I was ditching."

"Good." She turned to 'Bastian. "Where to?"

Out on the open sea, north of the Ghosts, Callahan shut off the *Bootstrap*'s engine, worrying briefly about his ability to restart it later. *Damn thing's been acting up.* He walked onto the deck and waited in the rain. *At least the bloody typhoon has passed.* His left hand gripped and regripped a small leather pouch inside his pocket.

Right on schedule, another cabin cruiser approached. Callahan strained to catch its markings, but as soon as it got close, the new boat flicked on a spotlight, shining it right in Callahan's face. Callahan shielded his eyes with his right arm. He tried to make out the figure behind the light, as the boat pulled alongside him. But all he could see was a dark male silhouette.

The silhouette called out, "Callahan?"

"Yeah. You, Setebos?"

"Yes."

"Shut off that light, mate; you're blindin' me."

"No. Do you have the *zemi*?"

Callahan was annoyed by the man's dismissive tone and prissy English accent. But the Aussie wasn't there to make friends. "I've got it."

"Toss it over. Carefully."

"Money first."

"Fine."

Callahan couldn't see but heard the thump of a package at his feet. He bent down, turning his back to the light and blinked a few hundred times until he could focus his eyes on the leather doctor's bag before him. He snapped it open. It was full of one-hundred-dollar bills. He took his time counting.

The voice called out: "The *zemi*, Mr. Callahan."

Callahan ignored him and continued his count. Finally, satisfied that his payment—*50K American*—had been received in full, he wheeled about quickly and tossed the leather pouch to the next boat. He saw two leather-gloved hands fumble for it, and half hoped that this Setebos would bobble the thing into the ocean. *Could charge a pretty penny to retrieve it all over again.* But the hands secured the pouch and removed the armband. The golden snakes caught the light.

The voice said, "And you're sure this is the original?"

"Yeah, of course." It was only after he spoke that a wave of doubt swept over Callahan. *The girl didn't . . . She couldn't have . . .* The doubts led him down a less than profitable path, so he quickly pushed them out of his head.

The voice betrayed some pleasure. "Good work, Mr. Callahan. One down. Eight to go."

"Same price."

"Yes."

"Same price for *each*?"

"Yes. And a bonus when we find the ninth."

"Ripper. Nice doing business with you Mr. Setebos."

But the other boat was already pulling away. The spotlight continued to blind Callahan until the fog had completely swallowed up light, boat and employer. Callahan stood there in the rain with the doctor's bag of loot tucked under his arm like a rugger ball. Then he nodded to himself. And took the *Bootstrap* back to harbor.

But that wasn't the only rendezvous of the night. It wasn't even the first.

What remained of Hurricane Julia—little more than a swirling, angry mist surrounding one weary eye— dragged itself onto Tío Sam's shores and coalesced into a human female with the clear intent—to us, anyway—of having another go at Rain, Charlie and 'Bastian, before—or more likely during—their crossing back to San Próspero. But Maq and I were on the beach, ready and waiting to intercept.

"That'll be a quarter," Maq said.

"What?" she said, staring him down with dark eyes that flashed anger and lightning.

"Every time you attack my people and fail, you owe me a quarter, *Hura-hupia*."

"Don't call me that."

"What else should I—"

"You know my name."

"Julia?"

"No, old man! I am . . ." She stopped herself. It's never wise to speak one's true name aloud. Even among old companions. You never know who *else* might be listening.

Maq chuckled, pushed his hat back on his head and waved the idea away. "I know who you *want* to be, *Hura-hupia*. But your wanting something doesn't make it so. As I believe tonight has demonstrated."

"The night isn't over."

"It is for you. You took your shot—the fourth in four nights, if I'm not mistaken?" Her scowl demonstrated he wasn't, so he forged on. "You took your shot. And they shot you down."

She looked from Maq to me, as if I might prove more sympathetic—or at least more reasonable. But I said nothing. If anything, I was far angrier with her than Maq was. He always excused her behavior on the pretext that she was following her nature. Only her methods made him shake his head.

"You wanna know the definition of crazy?" Maq asked.

"You?" she countered.

Maq chuckled again. "I like that. But I was thinking that crazy is trying the same thing over and over, and somehow expecting different results. Bringing down the plane didn't stop us all those years ago. Why assume it would tonight?"

"It would have worked all those years ago, if you hadn't cheated by pulling the Bohique out of the water."

"Sebastian made it to the surface on his own. That

merited reward in my book. So what if Opie and I pulled him into an old fishing boat and brought him to Tío Sam's? He wasn't even conscious. He never knew it was us. Sure, I may cheat. But I cheat fairly." She stared at him, appalled. And even I gave him a look over that one. But he was on a roll and waved us both off: "Point is, he beat you then. And they beat you again tonight."

She was on the verge of protesting once more that the night was young, but he'd have none of it. "I'm not telling you it's over," he said. "I'm just saying it's over for the evening. They've earned the next step. You attempt to interfere with that, and you'll have to face us."

"That prospect doesn't scare me, old man."

"It should. At least, it should tonight. You can pretend they didn't hurt you, weaken you, but we all know better. You're in no condition for direct confrontation."

"If you're so confident, why not end this now?"

"None of 'this' begins or ends with you, *Hura-hupia.* Besides, confrontation isn't my style. So don't push me. None of us would wake up happy. Or even again."

She glowered at him for a good nine seconds. For *exactly* nine seconds. Then she nodded. He responded by stepping aside. But I was less inclined. I bared my teeth and growled at her. To my mind, ending it now *did* have some appeal.

But Maq was already wandering off down the beach.

Julia was already forgotten. For all I knew, *I* was already forgotten within what passed for the old bum's mind. Embarrassed, I ran off after him, proverbial tail between my legs.

Then at the last moment, Maq turned and said, "Wait. She owes me a quarter." We both looked back. But she was gone.

CHAPTER EIGHTEEN

THE CACHE

The rain had finally stopped, and the moon, which had broken free of the clouds, shone brightly down upon Rain, Charlie and 'Bastian in the clearing. Everything smelled wet and clean and vaguely of bananas. A flamenco guitar played softly in Rain's head. She felt on the verge of yet another something new.

Charlie, on the other hand, was still having trouble fathoming the old. *How did we manage to get back here unscathed?* The thought of Callahan still scared him, and the memory of the flight overwhelmed him. So he focused on the little things: "I can't believe Miller, Dusanek—anyone—didn't ask us about the plane."

Rain smiled wryly. "Why would they? It's not like we could have possibly flown in on it, right?"

Charlie chuckled involuntarily. *No. Who would ever believe that?*

Both kids were still damp and shoeless, and mosquitoes buzzed around their ears. But 'Bastian was free of those plagues. He wandered toward the edge of the cliff. Rain turned to face him. "So your grandmother really brought you *here* . . . to the N.T.Z.?"

"It didn't have a name back then."

Charlie couldn't hear 'Bastian and was still lost in his own musings. He waved a couple bugs away and looked skyward. "The rain's stopped, and it's not so late. If we hang out long enough, I bet a party'll materialize."

"Then we better get to it," 'Bastian said, as he knelt beside a vine-covered section of the sandstone slab at the cliff's edge.

"Get to what?" Rain—followed by a meandering Charlie—approached him.

'Bastian reached toward the wiry green-brown strands, but stopped himself before his hand passed through them. The two kids stood over him. "Move the vines," he said. "They weren't here, and I remember . . ."

Rain crouched down and tore the vines free of the slab, revealing a circular indentation in the stone. 'Bastian nodded. "Like my *abuela* always told me: 'To unlock a door, you need two things . . .'"

Rain immediately understood. "'A key . . .'" she said, removing the entwined snakes from her arm, "'. . . and someone who knows how to turn it.'" She placed the armband in the indentation. *Perfect fit.* Then she twisted and removed the snake charm as she would the key to her locked bedroom door. She stood and stepped back as the sandstone block began to glow . . . to her and 'Bastian, at least.

The stone began to grind and move. Charlie backed away cautiously. 'Bastian did the same. The slab slid over to the side, revealing a set of stone steps descending down into the cliff and darkness.

In sarcastic unison, 'Bastian and Charlie said, "Gee, never saw that coming." Rain smiled at her companions and led them forward, padding down the cold stone stairs. 'Bastian followed, but so did Charlie, who walked right through the Dark Man, unaware. 'Bastian pulled up short, visibly annoyed to anyone who could see the dead. Then grunting to himself, he took up the rear.

The stairway was circular and close. Damp sandstone walls made it necessary to walk single file. The moon shining down from the entrance above and 'Bastian's soft glow were the only sources of light. Rain began to feel apprehensive again as the guitar in her head picked up the tempo. "It's getting pretty dark in here."

Suddenly, beside her, a torch flared to life, startling

all three of them. Rain glanced back at Charlie, smiled weakly, then continued down. He hesitated, staring at the flames. "Now that's service," he said. And then, "I'd like a cheeseburger." He paused, waiting.

Behind him, 'Bastian was growling impatiently, "Come on, kid, move it."

But Charlie couldn't hear him. Rather, he reacted to the lack of a magically materializing cheeseburger with a shrug and a "Worth a shot." He followed after Rain. "You ask for one."

She ignored him. She reached the bottom of the staircase and stepped down into a darkened hold. Another torch, to her right, flared to life. Then one by one, consecutive torches flamed on all around the stone room, shedding rich, flickering firelight on the ancient chamber. Now, Rain could see where she was: a wide expanse, cut into the cliffside. Along the wall to her right were one, two, three . . . nine stone seats carved out of the rock. Along the left was a long empty shelf, also carved out of the wall. And before her, there was no wall at all. Just a wide terrace, open to the elements, revealing nearly the same view of the ocean that one could see from the sandstone block at the edge of the N.T.Z.

Charlie and 'Bastian stepped off the stairs to either side of her. All three were pretty darn impressed. Charlie even whistled. "Now, this took some work." His whistle and his words bounced along the stone walls, echoing through the chamber. Fascinated, he walked past Rain to explore the room.

'Bastian shook his head in wonder and glanced back up the staircase. "What do you figure, we're about thirty feet below the clearing?"

Rain turned to him. "Have you been down here before?"

"No. Never. Didn't know it existed."

"So what do I do?"

"Rain, over here." It was Charlie. He was standing at the far end of the left wall. There were nine indentations in the otherwise smooth-carved rock shelf. The last one, the one he stood next to, looked vaguely skull-shaped. He ran his hand along the shelf, passing the other indentations: a deep widening groove, an oval ring, a larger more circular ring, a shallow cup, a semi-amorphous cross, a thick equilateral triangle, a small cylindrical hole. And finally another circular indentation matching the one from the N.T.Z. above. Rain and 'Bastian moved in to look. And Charlie said, "Looks like another keyhole to me."

Rain was still holding the snake charm in her hand. She took a deep breath and placed the armband in the indentation. Immediately, the charm began to glow— hot yellow, orange and red.

"It's glowing," Charlie said.

Rain stared at him. "You can see that?"

Charlie's eyes remained fixed on the snake charm. "Yeah, of course."

Our trio took a step back as the glow raced from the charm to the shelf and up the side of the wall behind it. The entire wall seemed to catch fire, flaring brighter and brighter until all three were shielding their eyes and Rain could feel the heat speed-drying her clothes and hair. Then the light waned until all that remained was a set of flaming letters. Words. A message:

BIENVENIDO, BUSCADORA, A LA CACHÉ.

BIEN HECHO. HAS ENCONTRADO EL PRIMER ZEMI.

COMO TÚ, ES EL BUSCADOR Y EL CURADOR.

COMO TÚ, TAMBIÉN ES EL PRIMERO DE NUEVE.

TENEMOS POCO TIEMPO Y SÓLO UNA OPORTUNIDAD PARA CURAR LA HERIDA.

ENCUENTRA LOS NUEVE. PARA TI Y PARA ELLOS SON LAS LLAVES QUE ABRIRÁN EL VERDADERO ACERTIJO DE LAS FANTASMAS.

Rain's eyes were wide, scanning quickly, trying to take it all in. On her left, 'Bastian was doing the same, but to her right, Charlie was clearly frustrated. "Wonderful. It's in Spanish. Translation, please."

Before she could respond, the flaming letters burnt out, but the words remained charred into the back wall. Rain's brain tried to keep up, to adjust to all these changes. Gearing up to translate for her friend was the least of her problems: "Uh . . . It says 'Welcome.' 'Welcome, Searcher, to the Cache.'" She looked around the stone cave. Loosely waved an arm at it. "I guess this place is 'the Cache.'"

"And I guess you're 'the Searcher,'" Charlie said with almost casual wonder.

Rain brightened with that epiphany. "Hey, yeah." Smiling, she refocused on the message. "It congratulates . . . *me* . . . for finding the first '*zemi*.'"

All three looked confused. Charlie asked, "What's a *zemi*?"

Rain looked at 'Bastian. He just shook his head and shrugged.

She said, "I don't know. Well . . . Wait a minute—" She looked down at the shelf, at the snake charm key still snugly stuck in its keyhole. "I guess this armband must be a *zemi*, whatever that means."

Charlie was getting impatient now, losing himself

finally in his curiosity and the quest. "What else does it say?"

Rain looked up again, reading and mentally making the simultaneous translation. "It says: 'You have found the first *zemi*. Like you, it is . . . the Searcher and the Healer. Like you it is also the first of nine.'"

'Bastian was stunned. "There are nine of these?"

Not hearing that, Charlie nevertheless responded. "I counted nine keyholes. They're all different shapes."

And Rain, "Every one?"

"Every one, yeah. Keep reading!"

Rain found her place again. "'We have little time and only one chance to . . .'" She paused, trying to decipher the next phrase.

'Bastian prompted her: "'Heal the wound.'"

"'Heal the wound . . . ?'" she repeated, unsure and frustrated. "I don't know what that means either." Failing to find any immediate answers, she shook off her confusion to finish the translation: "'*Encuentra los nueve*. Find the nine. For you and they are the Keys to unlocking the true Mystery of the Ghosts.'"

The three stood there in silence for a time as the phrase "Mystery of the Ghosts" echoed through the Cache. Rain looked around the chamber. At the nine stone chairs. At the nine keyholes. At the words, the walls, the torches flickering in the wind. At the night sky and the ocean in the distance. The room, the world, seemed very large, and the three of them felt very small in comparison. And yet, none of this made her unhappy.

'Bastian spoke. "Looks like we have another mission."

Rain nodded. "I've got to search out eight more of these . . . 'zemis' . . . and use them to heal some kind of wound before it's too late. . . ."

"Okay," Charlie said. "You twisted my arm. I'm in."

"Me too"—from 'Bastian.

Rain looked from one to the other. "Thanks. Both of you."

Rain lifted the snake charm out of its slot and slipped it back onto her arm. "Guess I'll need this for the next time we find a zemi."

"Plus," Charlie said, "it'd be cruel to strand 'Bastian down here."

Rain and the Dark Man exchanged a look. 'Bastian said, "I think he's getting the hang of this stuff."

And Charlie chuckled at his little joke. And 'Bastian chuckled at his own. And Rain giggled at the both of them. *Boys.*

CHAPTER NINETEEN

"Laissez les bontemps rouler . . ."

Rain, Charlie and 'Bastian climbed the carved steps up to the moonlit N.T.Z. As soon as they got clear, the sandstone block slid back into place quickly and automatically—with a heavy echoing thud as it found its home. "Glad it waited for us," Charlie said. Suddenly jokes about getting stranded in the Cache didn't seem so funny.

Rain thought her mind was playing a new song. Not just music. A song. Rock guitar, bass, and drums. A pounding beat and lyrics she couldn't quite make out. The volume kept increasing, so by the time she deciphered the refrain, *"Let the Good Times Roll . . ."* she knew the music wasn't coming from her head. It was approaching from the jungle.

Ramon Hernandez emerged into the N.T.Z. with a massive MP3-compatible boom box on his shoulder. He shouted back over the box and the blaring song, "See, there's someone here ahead of us!"

Like familiar spirits, local teens poured like smoke into the N.T.Z. Charlie's older brother Hank. Linda Wheeler. Jay Ibara. Renée Jackson. Marina Cortez. And more by the minute. Marina saw Rain and smiled at her, as Ramon leaned back and yelled to the heavens: "IT'S THE END OF SUMMERRRR!!!!! Time to PARTYYYYY!!!!"

Charlie exhaled loudly and leaned in to 'whisper' over the music to Rain, "Closed up that cache in the nick o'time, huh?" Rain didn't nod. Even in profile, he could see her eyes were shining, focused on new goals, a new world.

"... GOOD! TIMES! ROLL! LET THE GOOD TIMES ROLL!" Ramon cranked the music even louder and lowered the boom box onto a flat rock. Jay dumped the first armful of driftwood into the fire pit. Someone, maybe Hank, got it burning nearly as fast as those torches flamed to life below. More driftwood appeared, fueling the blaze, and soon the N.T.Z. was sporting a legitimate bonfire.

Rain, Charlie and 'Bastian watched the kids dance in their bare feet and shout at each other over the music. A big grin began to emerge on Rain's face, as she finally seemed to become aware of the party that had indeed materialized before her. Standing on her right, Charlie watched her turn left to make eye contact with oxygen. "C'mon. Let's dance," she said.

"You're kidding," the ghost replied.

"Can't a girl dance with her grandpa?"

The Dark Man smiled. "I don't see why not."

Getting the gist of their exchange, Charlie made a halfhearted effort to inject some reality: "Uh, Rain . . . You're overlooking . . ." But Rain rushed toward the crowd around the fire and joined the dance. Charlie sighed and shook his head. "Never mind. You two just have fun."

Rain danced with her grandfather. Young as he looked (to Rain) and felt (to himself), this wasn't really Old Sebastian's preferred style of music or movement. In addition, various teenagers kept inadvertently sticking various body parts right through him. Hank Dauphin literally jumped through the Dark Man's chest at one point. But 'Bastian made a conscious effort to ignore all of that, even made an honest attempt to mimic the moves of some of the other boys. He was quite deceased, but he felt very much alive, and one awkward dance seemed a cheap price to pay for the opportunity to see the non-supernatural glow radiating from his granddaughter.

Charlie was watching from the sidelines—completely annoyed that he was jealous of his platonic friend's dead invisible grandfather—when a semi-familiar voice said, "Hi," in his left ear. Charlie turned.

"Oh, Miranda, hi."

"Hi," she repeated. She turned toward the "dance floor" and, seeing Rain, wondered why Charlie was scowling here by the cliff alone. "Uh, Charlie . . . Why is Rain—"

"Dancing by herself?" Charlie heard the bitterness in his own voice and didn't like it.

"Uh, yeah."

Charlie looked back toward his friend, and Miranda watched his expression change. Anger quickly melted into genuine admiration. Smiling, he leaned in to Miranda and said, "Because, and trust me on this, she's the strangest person you're ever going to meet." Miranda shot him a confused look, and he laughed, adding, "But that's a good thing. Come on. If we dance next to her, she won't look like such a freak."

Miranda shrugged happily and slipped off her own shoes as he took her hand and towed her over to Rain's general vicinity. Rain glanced his way, and Charlie yelled, "You'll thank us in the morning." He tried to arrange things so that Rain appeared to be dancing with both of them, and he even adjusted Miranda's position so she wouldn't be situated where he guessed 'Bastian was.

More teens manifested from between the banana plants. The N.T.Z. was packed. Full of laughter and shouting and the tribal drums of current generations. Sparks from the bonfire sailed up toward heaven on a ferry of pungent smoke. Black and white ashes floated down, leapt and danced and lighted, resembling the mosquitoes that the smoke had driven away. From under the branch of a mahogany tree, I watched the ghost of Sebastian Bohique lean forward out of habit, so that his sly "voice" could be heard over the music. "School starts tomorrow. You still feeling trapped, Raindrop?"

Rain Cacique's eyes flared with their own fire. "No, I'm not trapped. . . . I'm the Searcher."

Belatedly, I realized my tail was wagging. Probably had *been* wagging for some time. *Well, so what?* I thought. *I'm not ashamed.* I had been feeling fairly trapped myself, these last few years. Now the Searcher was found, and the Search had finally begun. *So let it wag. Let the ol' tail wag!*

Read on for an excerpt from

SPIRITS
of
ASH AND FOAM

Coming Soon

CHAPTER ONE

DETRITUS

MONDAY, SEPTEMBER 8

I must have dozed off. With a start, I woke up beneath a mahogany tree to find the clearing deserted. Only minutes before, or so it seemed, the N.T.Z. had been packed with local teens celebrating the end of summer. Or celebrating *despite* the end of summer, I suppose. But now there wasn't a soul in view. Or a ghost, for that matter.

I got to my feet and stretched, arching my back and craning my neck. What had been a roaring bonfire was now a cold, wet fire pit, but there was no shortage of light. The nearly perfect circle of an almost full moon illuminated the nearly perfect circle of the clearing. I padded over to the sandstone slab at the edge of the cliff and looked out over the Atlantic. A heavy quilt of mist had descended upon San Próspero below. Competing smells—orchids and bananas and ozone from the storm that had passed through earlier—tickled my nose. Mostly, I was hungry.

I scoured the place to see if the kids had left anything behind, but half a corn chip does not a meal make.

So I took off, slipping under banana plants and into the dense jungle that surrounds the N.T.Z. Heading down Macocael Mountain, dodging low hanging vines and leaping over exposed roots, I passed "The Sign." I glanced back over my shoulder to confirm it hadn't changed. *Because,* as Maq is fond of saying, *in these parts, you never know, do you?* But the incongruous artifact remained a true constant: a stolen "PED X-ING" sign with two iconic pedestrian-tourists surrounded by a hand-painted red circle with a line through it. Above the figures, the hand-painted, slashing red initials **N.T.Z.** marked the hidden, semi-secret clearing above as a haven for local kids only. No Tourists Allowed in the No Tourist Zone.

Near the bottom of Macocael, I passed into the wet blanket of mist, and reaching Camino de Las Casas, paused to violently shake myself and fight off the damp. Then I trotted down the Camino toward Próspero

Beach. I knew Maq would be there, and I knew he'd have something for me to eat.

I wasn't wrong. (I rarely am.) Maq had a small driftwood fire going on the sand, which would have been lovely and warm, except he had constructed it ridiculously close to the incoming tide. A baby breaker spilled water into flame, extinguishing about half of the already minute blaze. But Maq didn't seem to mind. He cheerfully fed more driftwood into what remained of his fire and a nice piece of fresh snapper into my mouth.

"It's long after midnight, Opie," he said. "Where have you been?" But I was too busy wolfing down my meal to answer. Still, he seemed satisfied with that response and nodded sagely. I swallowed, and he said, "Want some more?"

Well, we are feasting tonight. I barked my approval, and he rubbed his knuckles across the yellow fur between my ears, while dropping another chunk of fish into the sand in front of me. I wagged my tail. *(Okay, yes, I'm canine. Get over it.)* Another wavelet sloshed into his shallow, struggling fire pit, as I snapped up the snapper.

Seconds later, I was bouncing around him like a *batey* ball, hoping for more—before realizing there was none. So I settled in beside my best friend and watched him contemplate the universe from beneath his straw hat. Maq stared down at the fire as the ocean finally put it out for good with an accompanying *hissss* and a cloud of steam, smoke and ash—all instantly carried off by a stiff breeze from the east. The water receded, leaving behind a layer of dirty sea foam amid the soaked coals, but the foam was quickly absorbed by the sand beneath. Maq, more pensive than I'm used to seeing him, considered this and nodded once again. "So many things are fleeting," he said, in that voice he had appropriated from W.C. Fields, back when the famous Hollywood actor had come to party on the Ghost Keys in 1935. "But even the most fleeting things return."

At first, I didn't have the slightest clue what he was talking about—but I was pretty sure he was talking about something. So I widened my perception beyond the beach, beyond the Pueblo, beyond San Próspero. And there, across the bay, I found what I was looking for on Sycorax Island: Isaac Naborías, bushy gray hair peeking out from under the hat of his official Sycorax Inc. security guard uniform, paused before the silent archeological excavation at the mouth of the old bat cave.

It was part of Isaac's lonely, four A.M. rounds: a trip about the old manor, past corporate headquarters, between the three factories and the cannery and then out to the dig and the cave—soon to be the site of a fourth factory. (*Or was it a second cannery?* Naborías wondered, none too sure.) Normally, he'd take a quick peek inside the cave, shine his heavy flashlight into its depths to make sure none of the late-shift employees were in there smoking anything funny. But just as he took a couple of shuffling steps toward the mouth, a lone bat flew out—right into his face. Naborías, eyes screwed shut, waved the thing away frantically; he *hated* bats! When he opened his eyes it was gone. He thought the exterminators the boss hired had taken care of those pests. Poisoned most of them and driven the rest away. Unfortunately, the cave was clearly still infested. He'd write that up in his nightly report, of course. That was his duty. But there was no way he was going inside there with those flying rats. So Isaac walked away in a huff—thus completely missing the bloodless, pale corpse lying face up, not five feet away on the dark, sandy floor of the cave.

CHAPTER TWO

MONDAY, SEPTEMBER 8

R ain Cacique's alarm clock woke her at six A.M. sharp. While Maq slept off the previous night on a bus bench, and I scratched at some sand fleas beneath it, Rain vaulted out of bed, excited to begin what she was convinced would be a brand new chapter in her life.

Quickly, she skittered into her bathroom, turned on the hot water, stripped out of her pajamas, and jumped in the shower. Steel drums played in her head, the morning's mental soundtrack: bright and warm, tangy and full of promise, just like her life since gaining . . . *it*.

As the near-scalding water rained down on her copper

skin, she touched the two golden snakes entwined around each other and around her upper left arm. One snake, the Searcher, had tiny chips of turquoise-colored stone for eyes; the other, the Healer, was sightless. Together, this armband of braided snakes—which for years she had seen her grandfather wear casually on his wrist—was the *zemi*. She wasn't exactly sure what a *zemi* was or even what the word *zemi* meant, but she knew the thing had mystic powers. The night before, the Healer snake had emitted a golden glow and mended a nasty scratch from a harpoon. *(A harpoon!)* And within the same hour, the Searcher snake had emitted a blue glow that helped save her, her best friend Charlie, and a whole bunch of ghosts from, well . . . from an evil, killer hurricane-woman! *Okay, yeah, it sounds crazy,* she thought, *but that's exactly what happened!* And she couldn't be more pleased. She soaped up, rinsed off, and was soon toweling dry in front of the mirror.

She stared into it, while brushing first her teeth and then her long black hair. She studied her face, staring into her almond-shaped, almond-colored eyes. She felt sure she should look different now—now that she had . . . super-powers. *I see dead people.* She giggled. Of course, the most important dead person in her life was her grandfather, her Papa Sebastian. But his ghost was somehow asleep inside the *zemi*, and wouldn't wake and emerge until sundown. And, oh, she couldn't wait until sundown.

She got dressed: panties, bra, khaki shorts, and a royal blue sleeveless tee with absolutely nothing imprinted on it that could label her as part of any circle, faction, or clique. She searched for her favorite shoes . . . and then remembered Charlie had been more or less forced to drop them overboard last night while they were trying to escape from that jerk Callahan. *The World's Most Dangerous Tourist* had stolen the armband, somehow knowing it was important even before Rain had figured things out. But Rain had stolen it back, leaving Callahan none the wiser. And now *she* knew it was the key to unlocking the ancient mystery of the Ghosts, the chain of eight islands on which Rain had spent her entire life—all thirteen years of it.

Was it only a few days ago she had felt so trapped? So completely locked into a tedious life of school and work, making beds and cutting bait for tourists, that would transition when she graduated into a tedious *eternity* of making beds and cutting bait for yet more tourists? Okay, sure, she still had school. In fact, today was the first day of the new year, the first day of eighth grade. But she could live with that, knowing what she now knew: the *zemi* wasn't the only Searcher/Healer.

Rain was also the Searcher and the Healer. She picked out another pair of deck shoes (honestly, she had like a hundred pairs anyway—well, okay, nine) and put them on. Then she began braiding her long, dark hair into the tight, thick rope she favored.

Relying on muscle memory alone, her fingers deftly danced the three lengths of hair into the braid, while her mind raced over all she had learned. Her *zemi*—a gift from her grandfather, who had himself received it as a gift from his *abuela* long ago—was only the first of nine *zemis* that she had to somehow search out and collect, so that she could heal a 'wound.' She had not a clue what the wound was, how she could heal it, or even where to look for the next *zemi*, but all those questions hardly weighed down her soaring thoughts now. Right now, all that mattered was the soaring. She didn't feel trapped in a small life anymore. She had real purpose, real responsibilities, and, ironically, that made her feel free. *The rest I'll figure out,* she thought. *I mean, one down, eight to go. How hard could it be?*

She pulled her backpack out of the closet and pulled her battered notebook off a shelf. It was jammed with notes from her various seventh grade classes. Without a moment's hesitation, she clicked open the binding and dumped every single sheet of used paper into the trash. Then she refilled it with a fresh, clean stack pulled from the plastic bag of school supplies she had purchased yesterday morning—a lifetime ago.

Also in the shopping bag were a couple new pencils, a couple new pens, a fluorescent yellow highlighter, a two-pocket folder for handouts and assignments, and a very old framed photograph of ten World War II airmen in front of their B-17 bomber, the *Island Belle*. She studied the photo for a moment or two. They were all dead now, except Old Joe Charone. There he was, decades ago, as an injured young tail-gunner. And there was Sebastian Bohique as a dashing young bomber pilot: not the old, warm, gray Papa 'Bastian she had known, worshipped, and loved—but a Dark Man with a very dangerous smile. And with 'Bastian and Joe, their crew: the Eight. All gone now. Released, at last, to their final rest, thanks to 'Bastian, Charlie, and herself. She carefully propped the picture up on her dresser and finished packing for school.

She exited her room, carefully locking the door behind her and double-checking to make sure. She didn't want any more unwelcome visitors lifting her stuff as Callahan had. Then with her backpack slung over one shoulder, she descended the front staircase of the only home she had ever known: the Nitaino Inn.

Her father, Alonso Cacique, was at the front desk, checking out the DeLancys and the Chungs. It was the standard routine: asking how their stay was, suggesting they recommend the Nitaino to their friends, etc. Rain was about to continue on to the dining room and kitchen to help her mom serve the breakfast portion of the Inn's Bed & Breakfast promise, when the front door opened, and a crowd of bodies noisily poured in.

She recognized Timo Craw, who led the way, hefting two very large rolling suitcases over the lip of the threshold. Timo was one of San Próspero's half dozen full-time cabdrivers, and, of course, Rain knew every local on the island. He was followed by an Asian woman in her mid-thirties, who—in addition to Sherpa-ing multiple airplane carry-ons—was trying to shepherd three very sleepy kids, ranging in age from eight to four. This brood was followed by their disheveled father, an Asian man about the same age as his wife. He also had two large rolling bags, which he had carried up the four cobblestone steps in front of the Inn, but which he had put down just shy of the doorframe. Now he was struggling to roll them over that last small speed bump with little luck or joy.

With a wiry grace, Alonso instantly slid out from behind the desk, dodging his slim but muscular six-foot form around a DeLancy here, a Chung there, etc., until he had reached the side of this newest *pater familias* and effortlessly taken charge of his bags. (*All those years working the charter boat had to be good for something,* Rain thought.) Alonso introduced himself as one of the Nitaino's proprietors, and the exhausted, somewhat befuddled but certainly grateful dad, shook his hand and said: "I'm Fred Kim. This is my wife Esther Kim. We're the Kims."

Alonso nodded to Rain, who knew the drill. While her dad did the heavy lifting, she crossed behind the desk and turned the register to face their new guests. "Hi, I'm Rain. I can check you in."

Esther Kim eyed the thirteen-year-old. "You work here?"

"Kinda have to. My folks run the place."

Mrs. Kim nodded and started to sign the guest book. Meanwhile, Timo had sized up the situation. The lobby of the Nitaino was generally considered large and warm and welcoming. But with four guests checking out, five checking in, plus a ton of luggage, two Caciques, a cabdriver, and a postcard rack, things had become decidedly cramped. To Timo Craw, that meant opportunity: "You folks need a ride to the airport? I got room fo' four."

John DeLancy and Terry Chung glanced at each other uncomfortably. John stammered: "Uh, w-we're n-not—"

"—Together," Terry finished.

Timo shrugged. "Sharing cab be cheaper, Captains. But it good with Timo either way. I take one couple now. Come back and take the other couple . . . sooooon as I can." Rain smiled at Timo's cheek. A second taxi could be there in five minutes easy. But the gamble paid off.

"Well, if it's cheaper," DeLancy said.

"Don't want to miss our flight," said Chung.

And so despite the dirty looks from Elizabeth Ellis-Chung and Ellen DeLancy, Timo was soon clearing some space in the lobby as he escorted the two couples and their luggage out the door—though not before Ms. Ellis-Chung had slipped an envelope into Rain's hand: her tip for serving breakfast, cleaning bathrooms, and making beds. Rain smiled and thanked her and watched her go.

The click of the door shutting behind them seemed to act as some kind of on-switch for the three Kim kids: the whining started instantly.

"I'm so tired . . ."

"What are we gonna do here anyway?"

"Mommy. Mommy. Mommy. Mommy. Mommy."

Mrs. Kim handed Rain her credit card and then turned to crouch before her kids: "I'm right here. I'm right here. I'm right here."

Rain ran the card immediately to secure the Kims' deposit *before* they could be told the inevitable bad news: check-in time wasn't until one P.M., and the two connecting rooms the Kims had reserved had only just been vacated by Timo's latest fares and weren't yet ready for occupation. Rain glanced down at the guest register and read the following names upside-down:

Rebecca Sawyer, Hannibal, MO
Mr. & Mrs. John DeLancy, San Francisco
Terry Chung and Elizabeth Ellis-Chung, Cambridge, Mass.
Callahan
Judith Vendaval, New York.
Fred, Esther, Wendy, John & Michael Kim. Seattle.

Wow, Rain thought, *they came all the way from Seattle! They must have been flying all night.* The inevitable bad news was going to be *really* bad news. She looked at the other names. Mrs. Sawyer and Ms. Vendaval were still staying at the Inn, but Callahan, *thank God,* was long gone.

At her first opportunity, Rain returned the credit card to Mrs. Kim and disappeared into the dining room—just as Alonso was saying, "You're going to have to give us a little time . . ."

Tourists. They were Rain's life—in fact, practically the sum total of her life until this past weekend. She lived with her parents in the Inn, which was almost never completely empty of guests. Among other chores, she served them breakfast, cleaned their rooms on weekends, and every couple weeks or so, helped crew her dad's charter boat for them. But all that had changed. Tourists had become a side venture. Her life now was with the *zemi*. And she wanted to shout it to the world.

Although maybe not to Rebecca Sawyer. The old woman was sitting alone in the dining room, reading a Lew Archer mystery novel and sipping black coffee. A half-eaten, fresh-baked scone sat on her bread plate. She glanced up over the top of her paperback and smiled. "Hello, Rain."

"Hi, Rebecca." The first morning after she had checked in, Mrs. Sawyer had insisted Rain call her Rebecca or Becky. Rain had settled on the more formal of the two options. "I'll have your breakfast in just a minute. Mom took your order?"

Mrs. Sawyer confirmed as much, and Rain passed through the swinging doors into the kitchen.

Instantly, she was hit by the wonderful smells of her mother's cooking. Iris Cacique had three skillets going on the burners. In one, she was sautéing onions, mushrooms, and tomatoes in salted butter, while flipping a half-cooked omelet in a second, and frying a few links of La Géante sausage in the third. There was a large bowl of mixed berries on the big wooden table where the family ate their own meals, alongside carafes of fresh orange and pineapple juice chilling in the ice bucket.

A cheerful Rain hung her backpack on the hook by the backdoor. "Morning!"

"Morning, baby," her mother said tenderly, glancing briefly at Rain, who could instantly tell Iris had been crying—and *not* because of the onions. For a second or two, Rain searched her brain for an explanation—and then it hit her: *'Bastian!* Her mother was still mourning her own father, who had only died three days ago. The funeral and the wake had followed rapidly, a Ghost Keys tradition, as it's not wise to let a body linger on a tropical island. But now life was supposed to go back to normal. *But what was the new normal?* Most days when Rain came down for breakfast, Papa 'Bastian was already sitting at the table, reading the paper and eating his Lucky Charms. But not today and not ever again. Of course, Rain knew that tonight—at sunset—'Bastian would emerge from the *zemi*, a bit pale, transparent, and ethereal but otherwise none the worse for being dead. But Iris didn't know that. Rain felt an irresistible longing to tell her mother. To tell her everything, the whole adventure—even the parts she knew would get her grounded for life. It was all so exciting, and she wanted to share it. *But how can I? She'll only think I'm nuts—or worse, on drugs or something.*

Rain settled for kissing her mom on the cheek and then setting up plates and spooning berries into a bowl, as Iris Cacique finished preparing Mrs. Sawyer's order.

"Anyone else out there?" Iris asked.

"Just Rebecca."

"That's a relief. I thought the Chungs or the De-Lancys might want something before hitting the road."

"They might've. But Timo rushed 'em out the door before they could think. Oh, but the Kims checked in early."

Iris growled under her breath. Rain smiled. That growl was very normal.

Two pieces of whole-wheat toast popped into view. A well-oiled machine, the Cacique women were on the job. Rain used two fingers to pluck the hot toast from the Inn's industrial toaster, dropping both on the bread-board. She sliced the pieces in half diagonally and arranged the two sets of triangles on a plate. Iris wheeled about with her saucepans, and soon the toast was joined by an onion-mushroom-tomato-and-jack omelet and sausage links. Rain was quickly through the swinging doors with the meal, serving Rebecca Sawyer with a smile. Seconds later, back in the kitchen, Rain was being asked what she wanted for breakfast.

"Actually, that looked really good."

Her mother's eyebrows raised a good half-inch in surprise. Iris Cacique's only child wasn't generally one for a big breakfast. But Rain was still flush with all the changes in her life. *A new day. A new way.* Besides, she had burned a *lot* of calories the night before, you know, fighting for her life and everything.

Iris started cooking again, and Rain poured herself half a glass of orange juice, topping it off with the same amount of pineapple. Iris asked: "You looking forward to eighth grade?"

Rain groaned, not so much because she dreaded school, but mostly because it seemed expected. Not that she *was* looking forward to it. Eighth grade would just get in the way of her new quest. After all, she was the Searcher and the Healer. *I should totally be exempt!* Suddenly, she remembered the form. She hopped up from the table and removed it from under the magnet on the fridge. "Mom, you still have to sign this."

Iris glanced back over her shoulder at Rain's Eighth Period Exemption Form. "I'll sign it if you want. But wouldn't you like to take an elective this semester? Photography, maybe?"

"Noooo. We talked about this. Work. Homework. It's enough. I need some free time—at least until volleyball starts."

"Right, because we wouldn't want you all *stressed out* from taking pictures of seashells and breakers, now, would we?"

"Mommmm."

"I said I'll sign it." And she did, after serving Rain's breakfast. Rain ate quickly, despite multiple pleas to slow down.

Iris cleared Rain's dishes, while Rain cleared Rebecca's—just as Alonso escorted the five Kims into the dining room. "Why don't you sit here, relax, have some breakfast—on the house—and we'll have your rooms ready by the time you're done eating."

Fred Kim grunted his acquiescence, while Esther Kim attempted to pour her seemingly liquid children into three chairs at one of the larger tables.

"I'm not even hungry."

"I want chocolate cereal."

"Mommy. Mommy. Mommy. Mommy. Mommy."

With a sigh of relief, Alonso followed Rain into the kitchen, only to be greeted by his wife's glare. "Tell me I did not hear the words 'on the house.'"

Rain watched her father stick his tongue into his cheek and take a deep breath to maintain his cool. "I've just spent twenty plus minutes arguing with Mr. Kim about his rooms not being ready. Hell, I could've *gotten* 'em ready in that time. I had to do something."

"Offering them breakfast, I understand. But they weren't supposed to check in until this afternoon. Breakfast is only served until ten."

"I know that."

"So why are they getting it for free? How are we supposed to earn a living if you keep giving away free food—especially when I'm the one who has to do the cooking."

Scooping up her form, Rain glided back from the tête-à-tête and quietly lifted her backpack off its hook. But not before her father shot a look her way. "Hold it, young lady. I need you to go strip the beds in rooms three and four before you leave."

"Gee, Dad. I'd love to. But you took away my master key."

And with that, she slipped out the back door before her exasperated father could formulate a reply.